THE
BUDDHA'S
RETURN

BUDDHA'S RETURN

Translated from the Russian by
Bryan Karetnyk

PUSHKIN PRESS

LONDON

Pushkin Press
71–75 Shelton Street, London WC2H 9JQ

The Buddha's Return was originally published in 1949–50
as *Vozvrashchenie Buddy* in the Russian-language journal
Novyi Zhurnal (*The New Review*), New York

This translation first published by Pushkin Press in 2014

ISBN 978 1 782270 59 1

The publication was effected under the auspices of the
Mikhail Prokhorov Foundation TRANSCRIPT Programme
to Support Translations of Russian Literature

transcript

Frontispiece: Gaito Gazdanov in the 1920s, Paris

Set in 10.25 on 13.75 Monotype Baskerville
by Tetragon, London

Proudly printed and bound in Great Britain
by TJ International, Padstow, Cornwall
on Munken Premium White 80gsm

www.pushkinpress.com

*We always act as if there were something
more valuable than human life.*

—ANTOINE DE SAINT-EXUPÉRY

I DIED. I have searched long and hard for the right words to describe what happened, and, convinced that none of the usual, familiar terms will do, have finally settled on one associated with what seems the least imprecise of realms: death. I died in the month of June, at night, during one of my first years abroad. This, however, was far less remarkable than my being the only person to know of this death, the only one to have witnessed it. I saw myself in the mountains; with that absurd invariable sense of urgency characteristic of events in which personal considerations for some reason cease to play any part, I found myself having to scale a high cliff with a sheer drop. Here and there little thorn-bushes somehow managed to cut through the brownish-grey rock surface; in places there were even dead tree trunks and roots creeping along rugged perpendicular clefts. Below, where I had begun my ascent, there was a low stone ledge skirting around the cliff, and lower still, in the dark abyss, was the distant muffled rumble of a mountain river. At length I climbed up, carefully groping for cavities in the stone and clinging now to a bush, now to the root of a tree, now to a jagged rock jutting out of the cliff face. I was slowly nearing a small shelf that had been obscured from below, but from which I somehow knew a narrow path led away; I couldn't shake off the oppressive and incomprehensible—like everything else that was going on—presentiment that I was destined nevermore to see it or to follow those narrow bends as it spiralled up unevenly, strewn with pine needles. Later, I remembered that I had sensed someone waiting for me up there, someone's keen, impatient desire to see me. I had at last almost reached the top; with my right hand I grabbed onto a pronounced stone ledge and in another few seconds I might have managed to pull myself up, when suddenly the solid granite crumbled beneath my fingers and I began to fall headlong, my body hitting the cliff face as the latter seemed to be soaring upwards before my eyes. Then came a sharp, almighty jolt that winded me and made the muscles in my arms ache—I was suspended in mid-air, my numb fingers clinging convulsively to the dried-out branch of a dead tree that had once nestled in a horizontal crevice in the rock. Below me was a void. I dangled there, my wide eyes transfixed by the patch of granite in my field of vision, as I sensed the branch steadily yielding beneath my weight. A small transparent lizard flashed for an instant a little above my fingers, and I distinctly saw its head, its flanks rising and falling rapidly, and its deathly gaze, cold and unmoving—a reptile's gaze. Then in one agile, elusive movement it darted upwards, vanishing. Shortly thereafter I heard the intense buzzing of a bumblebee, rising and falling in pitch, although not without a certain insistent melodiousness in some way resembling a vague acoustic memory, which I expected to crystallize at any moment. But the branch gave more and more under my fingers, and the terror penetrated deeper and deeper inside me. Least of all did this terror lend itself to description; what prevailed was an understanding that these were the final moments of my life, that no power on earth could save me, that I was alone, utterly alone, and that beneath me in those abysmal depths, which I could sense with every sinew of my body, death awaited me, and I was powerless against it. Never before had it occurred to me that these feelings—loneliness and terror—could be experienced not only mentally, but literally with every fibre of one's being. And although I was still alive and there was not a single scratch on my body, I was, at a phenomenal speed which nothing could halt or even slow, undergoing such mental agony, such chilling languor and insurmountable anguish. Only at the very last second, or even fraction of a second, did I feel something like sweet sacrilegious exhaustion, curiously inseparable from the languor and anguish. It seemed to me that if I were to combine into a single entity every sensation I had experienced over the course of my life, the collective power of these would still pale in comparison with what I had experienced in these past few minutes. But this was my final thought: there was a snap, the branch broke, and around me the rocks, bushes and ledges began spinning with such unbearable speed, until finally, after an eternity, amid the humid air there came the heavy crunch of my plummeting body hitting the rocks on the riverbank. A moment later I watched helplessly as the image of the sheer cliff and the mountain river disappeared before my eyes; then it was gone, and nothing remained.

Such was my recollection of death, after which I mysteriously continued to survive, if I am to assume that I did in fact remain myself. Prior to this, as with the majority of people, I had often dreamt that I was falling, but each time I had awoken during the fall. Yet as I made this arduous ascent to the top of the cliff, and when I met the cold gaze of the lizard, and when the branch broke beneath my fingers, I was aware that I was not asleep. I have to say that throughout this vivid and frankly banal incident, devoid as it was entirely of any romantic or chimeric nuances, there were two people present—a witness and a victim. This duality, however, was barely noticeable, at times imperceptible. And so, having returned from oblivion, I once again found myself in the world where until now I had led such a notional existence; it was not that the world around me had changed all of a sudden, but rather that I couldn't tell, amid the disorderly and random chaos of memories, unfounded concerns, contradictory emotions, sensations, odours and sights, what it was that demarcated my own existence, what belonged to me and what to others, and what was the illusive significance of that unstable compound of various elements, the absurd amalgam of which was theoretically supposed to constitute my being, imparting to me my name, nationality, date and place of birth, my personal history, which is to say that long sequence of failures, accidents and transformations. I felt as though I were slowly re-emerging, in the very place where I was never supposed to return—having forgotten everything that had taken place before now. But this wasn't amnesia in the literal sense of the word: I had just forgotten irrevocably what one was supposed to consider important, and what insignificant.

I could now sense the strange illusoriness of my own life everywhere—an illusoriness that was many-layered and inescapable, irrespective of whether it had to do with projects, plans or the immediate material conditions of life, all of which had the ability to change entirely over the course of a few days or a few hours. In any case, I had been acquainted with this state for some time; it was one of the things I hadn't forgotten. For me, the world consisted of objects and sensations that I recognized—as if I had experienced them long ago and only now were they coming back to me, like a dream lost in time. This had even been the case when I encountered them probably for the very first time in my life. It seemed as if, amid an enormous, chaotic combination of vastly disparate things, I had blindly sought the path I had trod before, without knowing how or where. Perhaps this is why the majority of events left me entirely indifferent and only a rare few moments containing—or seeming to contain—some sort of coincidence arrested my attention with incredible force. It would be difficult for me to pinpoint how exactly these moments differed from others—some inexplicable nuance, some random detail that was plain for me to see. They almost never influenced my own fate or personal interests directly; they were visions that usually appeared out of the blue. There had been years when my life somehow clearly didn't belong to me, and I took only an external, insignificant role in its events: I was entirely indifferent to what went on around me, despite there having been tempestuous scenes, sometimes involving mortal danger. But I understood this danger only theoretically, and I could never fully appreciate its true meaning, which would prob-ably have struck terror in my soul and compelled me to live other than I did. It often seemed to me—when I was alone and there was no one to prevent me from immersing myself in this endless series of vague sensations, visions and thoughts—that I lacked the strength for one last push, in order to discover myself and suddenly to comprehend at long last the hidden meaning of my destiny, which had until now been going through my memory like some hap-hazard relay of random occurrences. But I never managed to do this, nor did I even manage to comprehend why one thing or another, on the face of it bearing no relation to me whatsoever, would suddenly take on such a significance that was as incomprehensible as it was plainly apparent.

Now began a new phase in my life. A whole series of oddly powerful sensations, many of which I had never before experienced, passed through my very being: an unbearable thirst and the heat of the desert, the icy waves of a northern sea that surrounded me and in which I would spend hours swimming towards a far-distant rocky shore, the burning touch of a swarthy female body that I had never known. Often I endured torturous physical pain symptomatic of incurable diseases whose descriptions I would later find in medical textbooks—diseases from which I never suffered. I had gone blind more than once, I had been left crippled many times over, and one of the rare physical pleasures known to me was that of regaining consciousness and realizing that I was in the fullest of health and that due to some incomprehensible convergence of events I was now beyond these excruciating states of sickness or injury.

Of course, it was far from always the case that I had to endure such things. What had now become utterly immutable was a peculiarity owing to which I felt almost like a stranger to myself. Whenever I happened to be alone, I would be engulfed instantly by the troubled movements of a vast, imaginary world; it would hurtle me along uncontrollably and I would scarcely be able to keep pace with it. There was visual and auditory chaos, comprised of an array of disparate elements; sometimes it would be the music of a distant march, ensconced on all sides by high stone walls; sometimes it was the silent motion of an endless green landscape, broken only by the rolling hills and their strange undulation; sometimes it was the outlying environs of a Dutch town with stone troughs of uncertain origin, where the water trickled with a steady murmur—to intensify this obvious infringement of Dutch realism, women would go to them, one after another, carrying jugs on their heads. Nowhere was there any logical pattern in this, and the shifting chaos clearly failed to present even a remote semblance of any harmonious order. And so, accordingly, at that point in my life, which was marked by the constant attendance of chaos, my inner existence acquired an equally false and wavering character. I could never be certain how long any one feeling would last, I never knew what would come to replace it the very next day or in a week's time. And just as I had been amazed to learn upon reading my first books, after having mastered the alphabet, that the people there managed to speak in full sentences, using classical constructions of subject and predicate with a full stop at the end—although it seemed to me that no one ever did this in reality—so too it now appeared almost inconceivable to me that one person or another could be an accountant or a minister, a labourer or a bishop, and remain firmly convinced that his work was more important and enduring than anything else, as if a bishop's cassock or a labourer's jacket mysteriously but exactly corresponded to the personal calling and vocation of the man who wore it. I knew, of course, that within a given timeframe and under normal circumstances a labourer would never become a bishop, just as a bishop would not turn into a labourer, and often this state of affairs would last until death set them equal with grim indifference. Yet I also sensed that the world in which the former was fated to be this, and the latter that, could suddenly turn out to be notional and illusory, and that everything could alter beyond recognition. In other words, the arena in which my life unfolded was for me devoid of any clearly defined and in any way concrete features; there was nothing constant about it—the objects and ideas that comprised it could change in form and content, like the impossible metamorphoses of a never-ending dream. And each morning, upon waking, I would gaze with troubled wonderment at the wallpaper patterns in my hotel room, which always seemed different from the night before, because so many changes had occurred between yesterday and today, and I knew instinctively that I too might have changed, swept up by that imperceptible and irresistible motion. I seemed to be living in an almost abstract world, never quite managing to uncover the logic behind certain objects and concepts that had seemed so crucial and definitive to a number of my former teachers, a sort of fundamental law of all evolution and human existence.

It was in these distant and neurotic times that I met a man who seemed to have been summoned out of inexistence with the sole purpose of appearing before me at this precise stage in my life. Strictly speaking, he was not a man, but the unrecognizable, distorted spectre of someone who had once been alive. That man was no more, he had vanished, but not without trace, as there yet remained what I saw when the figure first approached me and said:

*"Excusez-moi de vous déranger. Vous ne pourriez pas m'avancer un peu d'argent?"**

His face was dark and covered in thick grey-and-ginger stubble, his eyes were swollen and his eyelids sagged; he wore a frayed black hat, a long jacket that looked like a short overcoat, or a short overcoat that looked like a very long jacket, dark grey in colour, black-and-whitish boots that were split all along the seams, and light-brown trousers covered in myriad specks of dirt. His eyes, however, looked ahead calmly and lucidly. But it was his voice that particularly struck me, being quite out of keeping with his appearance—a flat, deep voice, with an astonishing hint of confidence. It was impossible not to detect the echo of some other world, and not the one to which this man so

* I'm sorry to bother you. You couldn't lend me a little money, could you?

16

evidently belonged. No vagrant or beggar should have, or has indeed ever had, the ability or the right to speak in such a voice. And if I had required irrefutable evidence that this man was himself the living spectre of another, someone who had vanished, then these intonations and this acoustic revelation would have proved more convincing than any biographical testimony. It immediately made me pay much more attention to him than I would have done to a common tramp asking me for alms money. The second factor that piqued my interest was his unnaturally correct French.

The encounter took place towards the end of April, in the Jardin du Luxembourg; I was sitting on a bench, reading notes on Karamzin's travels. He fleetingly glanced at the book and launched into Russian—a very pure and correct Russian that preserved, incidentally, a few archaic turns of phrase: "I should consider it my duty", "if you would deign to take into account". Within a very short space of time he had divulged to me a number of details about himself that seemed no less fantastic than did his appearance; among these figured the misty buildings of the Imperial University in St Petersburg, where at one point he had studied, the Faculty of History, and some vague, cagy allusions to vast wealth, which he either had lost, or else was due to receive.

I extracted a ten-franc note and handed it to him. He bowed, maintaining an air of dignity that was perfectly out of place, and lifted his hat with a sort of undulating gesture, the likes of which I had never before seen. Then he walked off unhurriedly, carefully alternating his feet cased in their torn boots. Even in his back, however, there was none of that timid restraint or physical indignity symptomatic of people of his sort. Slowly he receded farther and farther into the distance; the April sun was already setting, and my imagination, running a few minutes ahead of itself like a bad watch, had already projected along the railings of the Jardin du Luxembourg the twilight that was to come a little later, but was absent at the time. And so this image of a beggar remained fixed in my memory, shrouded in the dusk that was yet to set in; the figure moved off and dissolved amid the milky softness of the outgoing day, and in this state, neurotic and illusory, it prompted several images in my mind. I later recalled that I had seen such light—light in which the last, just-departed ray of sun seems to have left a subtle though unmistakeable trace of its unhurried dissolution in the air—in a number of paintings, in particular one of Correggio's, although I was unable to remember which.

Yet for me these efforts of memory were transforming imperceptibly into something else, something no less customary, but recently more intense: an endless sequence of haunting visions. I would see a woman in a black dress buttoned up to the neck trudging along a narrow street in a mediaeval town, a thickset man wearing spectacles and

European clothes, lost and unhappy, searching for something he could not find, a tall, elderly man walking down a winding, dusty road, and a woman's wide, terror-stricken eyes set in a pale face that was somehow very familiar to me. Simultaneously I would experience strange, distressing sensations that mingled with my own feelings on some event or other in my life. And I noticed that some states of mind triggered by very definite factors would persist long after their causes had disappeared, and so I would ask myself what actually came first—the cause or the state of mind; and if the latter, then did it not in certain circumstances predetermine something irrevocable and substantial, something belonging to the material world? Besides, I was faced with yet another persistent question: what was it that connected me to these imaginary people whom I had never wittingly invented and who would appear to me so unexpectedly—like the one who had fallen from the cliff, in whose body I had died not so long ago, like that woman in black, like those others undoubtedly lurking ahead, eagerly waiting to embody me for a few brief, illusory moments. Each of them had been unlike the one that followed, and it was impossible to confuse them with one another. What tied me to them? The laws of heredity, whose lines criss-crossed in such fantastical arabesques all around me, someone's forgotten memories that were for some unknown reason being dredged up within me, or was it that I was part of some vast human collective and the impenetrable membrane that separated me from other people and contained my individuality had suddenly lost its impermeability, allowing something foreign to rush in, like waves crashing into the crevice of a cliff? I was unable to tell anyone about this, knowing that it would be taken for delirium or some peculiar form of madness. But it was neither of these. I was perfectly healthy, every muscle in my body responded with an automatic precision, I found none of my university courses in any way difficult, and my logical and analytical faculties were fine. I had never experienced fainting fits and I knew almost no physical fatigue: I was built, as it were, for the real world. Yet there was another—illusory—world that pursued me everywhere, hounding me. And nearly every day, sometimes in my room, sometimes in the street, in the woods or in the garden, I would cease to exist—I as such-and-such a person, born in such-and-such a place, in such-and-such a year, having completed my secondary education only a few years ago and attending lectures at such-and-such a university—and with peremptory inevitability, someone else would take my place. This metamorphosis would usually be preceded by torturous physical sensations, sometimes taking over the entire surface of my body.

I remember waking up one night and distinctly feeling my long, greasy, rank hair against my face, the slackness of my jowls, and the curiously familiar sensation of my tongue touching the gaps in my mouth where I was missing teeth. Seconds later, however, the awareness that I was merely a spectator in all this, as well as the heavy odour I had detected from the outset, would vanish. Then slowly, like a man gradually beginning to distinguish objects in the half-light—which, incidentally, was typical at the start of almost all these visions—I would discover this next distressing incarnation, the victim to which I had now fallen. I saw myself as an old woman with a tired, haggard body, deathly pale in colour. Through a small window overlooking a dark, narrow courtyard the oppressive stench of a deprived neighbourhood blew into the room in sultry summer waves; amid the suffocating heat this decrepit body, by whose sides drooped long, fleshy breasts and whose stomach with its roll of fat concealed the origin of two equally chubby legs that ended in black ragged toenails, lay on a grey-and-white bed sheet that was damp with sweat. Sound asleep next to it, head thrown back, mouth agape and white teeth bared, like a dog, was an Arab boy with tight thick curls of black hair, whose back and shoulders were covered in pimples.

The image of this old woman did not, however, occupy my mind for long. She gradually faded into the semi-darkness, and once again I found myself on my narrow bed, in my room with its high window overlooking a quiet street in the Latin Quarter. In the morning, when I awoke and opened my eyes again, I saw—this time entirely as a spectator to the event—that the Arab boy was gone, and on the bed remained only the corpse of the old woman, the sheets stained with dried blood from a terrible wound at her neck. I never saw her again: she disappeared for ever. But this was undoubtedly the most repulsive sensation I had ever experienced in my life—this body, fat and sagging, in such a cruel state of muscular incapacity.

Since the day that I first met the Russian beggar in the Jardin du Luxembourg, so clearly and indelibly etched in my memory—the black frayed hat, the stubble on his face, the tattered boots and that amazing garment, be it an overcoat or something resembling a jacket—nearly two years had passed. For me these had been long, almost endless years, filled with swarms of silent, delirious visions that blended corridors leading God knows where, narrow chasm-like vertical shafts, exotic trees on the far-distant shores of a southern sea, black rivers that flowed into dreams, and an uninterrupted stream of various people, both men and women, the reason for whose appearance invariably eluded my comprehension, but who were inseparable from my own existence. Nearly every day I would feel this almost abstract psychological weariness, the result of some manifold, unrelenting madness that curiously affected neither my health nor my faculties—nor even did it prevent me from sitting the occasional exam or memorizing a host of university lectures. Sometimes this noiseless torrent would come to a sudden halt without any forewarning whatsoever; I was drifting through life then without a care in the world, breathing in the damp winter air of the Parisian streets and with carnivorous zeal devouring plates of meat in restaurants, tearing at the succulent morsels with my voracious teeth.

On one such day I was sitting at a table in a large café on the Boulevard du Montparnasse, drinking coffee and reading a newspaper. Behind me, an assured male voice, evidently concluding—judging by his final intonation— some period that I hadn't heard, said:

"And believe me, I have enough experience in life to know."

I turned around. There was something familiar about his voice. However, the man I saw was completely unknown to me. I quickly looked him over: he was wearing a fitted overcoat, a shirt with a starched collar, a deep-crimson tie, a navy-blue suit and a gold wristwatch. A pair of spectacles rested on his nose, and there was a book lying open in front of him. Next to him sat a blonde woman of around thirty, an artist whom I had met a few times at evenings hosted by some friends; she was puffing away on a cigarette and seemed to be listening to him distractedly. He then closed the book and took off his glasses—he was evidently far-sighted—and that was when I saw his eyes. To my utter disbelief, I recognized the man to whom I had given the ten francs in the Jardin du Luxembourg. I could never have identified him solely on the basis of his eyes and his voice, though, for the man sitting here in the café seemed to have nothing in common with the beggar who had approached me two years ago, asking for money. Never before had it occurred to me that clothes could so change a man. There was something unnatural and implausible about his metamorphosis. It was as if time had fantastically regressed. Two years ago this man had been a mere shadow; now he had miraculously transformed back into the man he had once been, whose disappearance ought to have been irreversible. I was unable to come to my senses for genuine astonishment.

The female artist got up to leave, waving to me both hello and goodbye simultaneously as she made her exit. Then I went up to the gentleman's table and said:

"Forgive me, but I believe I've had the pleasure of meeting you somewhere before."

"Please, do sit down," he replied with quiet courtesy. "It's a credit to your memory. You're the first of those who knew me in the old days to have recognized me. You say we've met? You're quite correct. It was back when I was living in a slum, in Rue Simon le Franc."

He made a vague hand gesture.

"I presume you would like to know what happened to me? Well then, let us begin with the fact that miracles simply do not happen."

"Until a few moments ago I'd have agreed with you, but now I'm beginning to wonder."

"Oh, you'd be wrong to doubt it," he said. "There's nothing more deceptive than appearances. One can make assertions on the basis of these only if one acknowledges their total arbitrariness beforehand. In five minutes' time the causes of my metamorphosis will seem entirely natural to you."

He leant his elbows on the table.

"I don't recall whether I told you back then…"

And so he told me exactly what had happened to him, and truly there was nothing miraculous about it. In one of the Baltic states—he neglected to mention which—lived his elder brother, who, in the wake of the Revolution, had managed to retain a sizeable fortune. According to my acquaintance, he was a cruel and miserly man, who hated everyone who had, or might have had, cause to ask him for money. He never married and he had no heirs. Some time ago he had drowned while bathing in the sea, and so the inheritance passed on to his brother, whom a solicitor tracked down in Paris, living in Rue Simon le Franc. Once the formalities had been concluded, he came into possession of a fortune valued at many hundreds of thousands of francs. Then he took an apartment on Rue Molitor, living alone and passing the time, as he put it, between reading and pleasant idleness. He invited me to drop by one day between appointed hours; there was no need to call in advance. Thereupon we parted. I stayed on in the café, and again, just as I had done two years ago,

I watched him leave. It was April, but the day was cold by comparison with the previous year. He walked along the wide passage between the little café tables and slowly vanished into the soft electric light in his new fitted overcoat and new hat; now the assuredness of his gait could seem in no way out of place to anyone, even to me, who had been so struck by it at our first meeting.

Alone, I lapsed into thought—contemplative at first and without aim; then, among the formless motion of images, features gradually drew into focus and I began to recall the events that had taken place two years ago. Now it was cold, but then it had been warm, and I had remained sitting on that bench in the Jardin du Luxembourg, just as I did now in the café, following the man's departure. Back then, of course, I had been reading Karamzin: immediately forgetting the words on the page, my thoughts kept returning to the nineteenth century and its sharp disparity with the twentieth. I even pondered the differences in political regimes—thoughts that, generally speaking, very seldom captivated my attention—and it seemed to me that the nineteenth century had known none of the barbaric and violent forms of government that characterized the history of certain nations in the twentieth century. I recalled Durkheim's theory of "social constraint", *contrainte sociale*, and, deviating once again from the university's course material, I proceeded to considerations of a more general and more contentious order. I mused on the idiocy of state-led violence and how it ought to have been much more apparent to contemporaries than to so-called "future historians", who would fail to grasp the personal tragedy of this oppression, along with its palpable absurdity. I also thought how state ethics, taken to their logical paroxysm—as the culmination of some collective delirium—would inevitably lead to an almost criminal notion of authority, and that, in such periods of history, power truly belongs to ignorant crooks and fanatics, tyrants and madmen: sometimes they end their life on the gallows or at the guillotine, sometimes they die of natural causes, their coffin accompanied on its journey by the unspoken damnation of those whose misfortune and disgrace it was to be their subjects. I also thought of the Grand Inquisitor and the tragic fate of his author, and how personal, even illusory freedom can essentially prove to have a negative value, with a meaning and significance that frequently eludes us because it contains, in an extremely unstable equilibrium, the roots of opposition.

But now I was far from such thoughts; they seemed obscure and insignificant by comparison with the egotistical considerations of my own destiny, the illusory and uncertain nature of which had never ceased to captivate my attention, all the more so as today's encounter had coincided with the demise of this happy phase of my life, the blessedness—I could find no other word for it—of which lay in the fact that during these past few weeks I had lived without dreaming and without thinking about anything.

The previous day I had been seized by a vague sense of anxiety, inexplicable as always and for that very reason particularly troubling. The next day the feeling intensified, and now it no longer left me. It began to seem to me as if some danger, intangible and unfathomable in equal measure, were lurking in the wings. Had I not been so used to the constant presence of this hallucinatory world that so doggedly pursued me, I might perhaps have been frightened that this was the onset of some persecution complex. Yet the singularity of my situation resided in the fact that, as opposed to people afflicted by genuine madness, those utterly convinced that some invisible, elusive figure truly was following them—someone with a multitude of agents at their disposal: a bus conductor, a laundress, a policeman, a strange gentleman in spectacles and a hat—I knew that my unease could be attributed wholly and exclusively to random flights of imagination. Living as I did, with almost no independent means at my disposal, unaffiliated with any political organization, partaking in no form of social activity and in no way distinguishing myself from the anonymous multimillion mass of the Parisian public, I knew there was no way I could be the object of anyone's pursuit. There was not a single person in existence to whom my life could have presented any interest, no one who could have envied me.

I understood perfectly that my vague anxiety was entirely pointless, that there were and could be no grounds for it. Yet as inconceivable as it was, still the feeling persisted, and the fact that it was clearly unfounded failed to extricate me from this situation. Meanwhile, in contrast to maniacs, whose attention is strained to breaking point, who never miss a single detail of what is happening around them as they resolutely seek out the presence of their pursuant adversary, I lived and moved as if surrounded by a thin veil of fog, one that deprived objects and people of their sharply defined contours.

I would fall asleep and awake with this feeling of vague unease and foreboding. Days went by like this, and the feeling persisted until the moment when, in the twilight of a Parisian evening, while wandering aimlessly through the streets in an unfamiliar part of the city, I cut down a narrow passageway between two buildings. By now it was almost completely dark. The alley turned out to be surprisingly long, and when I reached the end I found myself standing in front of a blind wall, with a left turn leading off at right angles. I carried on, presuming a way out to be round the corner, but it grew even darker. As I walked between the two walls, I could just make out that one of them had been built with niches at regular intervals. Their purpose was a mystery to me. I continued another few dozen metres in the gloomy darkness, above which was a starless sky; there was total silence, broken only by the sound of my own footsteps along the uneven paving. Suddenly, as I drew abreast of one of the niches I had spotted earlier, without a sound a man's black shadow leapt out in front of me with extraordinary speed, and for a brief fraction of a second I experienced that mortal terror for which this unrelenting state of disquiet had prepared me over the course of many days. I then felt at my neck the vicelike fingers of the man who had so suddenly and unaccountably lunged at me. As strange as it may seem, from that moment on I ceased to feel any abstract unease or immediate terror. Then again, I had no time for it. Now amid the action there was something concrete and tangible; there was reality, not irresistible abstraction. Instinctively I tensed the muscles in my neck. Judging by the frantic clutch of fingers at my throat, it was obvious that they belonged to a strong adult male, who moreover had the element of surprise on his side. However, it was also clear to me that despite the apparent superiority of his position and the desperation of my own, the advantage ultimately lay with me. I comprehended this in the very first seconds; I was well trained in various types of sport, particularly combat, and I had no difficulty in determining that my assailant knew nothing of this and only hoped to rely on brute strength. He was probably expecting me to grab him by the hands and attempt to prise them from my neck—the natural and most often useless defence of the unprepared man. By now already choking, however,

I groped in the dark for his two little fingers, and then simultaneously, using both my hands, I bent them back sharply, breaking their lower joints. He gasped and started to groan, and my breathing strangely eased after he let go of my throat. He was now silently writhing about in front of me in the darkness, and at any other time this would no doubt have roused some compassion in me. But I was in a state of sudden, furious rage—as if this unidentified man had been the cause of that lengthy unease that had tormented me all this time, as if he himself were the culprit. I pressed into one of his shoulders while at the same time pulling the other one towards me, and when, without his having the time to realize what was happening, he turned away from me, I seized his neck from behind using my right arm bent at almost ninety degrees. With the fingers of my left hand I grasped my right wrist and began to tighten my deadly grip on him, not letting up for an instant. In short, I did what he ought to have done when trying to strangle me—precisely what he had failed to do, thus signing his own death warrant. He twitched a few times, although I knew that his situation was hopeless. Then, once all trace of resistance had vanished, I let go and his corpse slumped heavily to my feet. It was so dark that I was unable to examine his face properly. I noted only that he had a little moustache and black curly hair.

I listened intently. Around me, as before, there was total silence, and as I took my first step the sound of it seemed alarmingly loud. Without looking back, I continued along the passageway. At last the indistinct light of what was probably a street lamp glinted in the distance, and I heaved a sigh of relief. However, just as I was about to leave this trap something struck me on the head with tremendous force, and I lost consciousness.

Through this blackout, I had the vague notion that I was being driven somewhere. Clearly I had been administered with some powerful narcotic, as my unconscious or semi-conscious state was unnaturally prolonged. When I finally opened my eyes, I found myself lying on a narrow stone bench in a small room with a high ceiling and three grey walls. There was no fourth wall: in its place shone a bright gaping hole. I had completely lost all concept of time. On the other side of a blind wooden door I could hear footsteps and voices shouting things that I was unable to make out. These voices soon receded into the distance. I looked around the cell and only then did I notice that I was not alone: to my right, on a second stone bench, was a figure clothed in rags, sitting with his legs crossed and leaning against the wall. His eyes were closed, but his lips moved silently. He then turned his head to me and slowly lifted his eyelids; I met his gaze—penetrating, empty and cold, so much so that I immediately felt out of sorts. I remembered everything after this exactly as it happened with the exception of one detail, which no effort of memory could ever return to me: I couldn't remember in which language I had spoken, at first with him, and then with all the others. Some phrases seemed to have been uttered in Russian, others in French, others in English or German.

"Permit me to welcome you," said the man in rags, whose dull, inexpressive voice immediately struck me. "I haven't the pleasure of knowing your name."

I introduced myself and asked whether he could explain where I was and what I was doing here.

"You've been remanded in custody."

"Remanded in custody?" I repeated in astonishment. "But on what grounds?"

"The relevant charges will likely be brought against you in the near future—what they are precisely, I don't know."

An enormous bird with a bald neck slowly flew past the bright aperture in the wall, almost brushing it with its wing. Its appearance here, coupled with the replies of my interlocutor, seemed so improbable that I asked:

"What country is this?"

"You are in the territory of the Central State."

For some reason I found this answer satisfactory; this was probably because of the effect of the narcotic not yet having completely worn off. With an effort, I got to my feet and took a few steps towards the opening—evidently in lieu of a window—and instinctively recoiled: it gave onto a courtyard, but the cell was unusually high up, probably on the thirtieth floor. Opposite the building, separated by a distance of forty or fifty metres, was a solid wall.

"Escape is impossible," said my companion, who had been following my every move.

I nodded. Then I told him that I refused to recognize the reasons for my being held here, that I was guilty of no crime and all this was utterly absurd. Next I asked him why he had been arrested and what lay in store for him. Then for the first time he smiled and replied that in his case there had been a clear misunderstanding and that he would personally face no punishment.

"But what exactly happened to you?" he asked.

I related to him in great detail the little-convincing facts that had led me here so unexpectedly. He asked me a few more pieces of information about my life and, having heard me out, said that he was entirely satisfied by my account and would advocate my release. Such a statement ought to have seemed at least a little strange coming from a prisoner in rags. However, I took him at his word; my analytical faculties had not yet returned to me.

After a while the door to the cell opened, and two armed soldiers, one of whom barked out my surname, escorted me down a long corridor with pink walls and a multitude of turns. At each turn hung the same enormous portrait of some elderly, clean-shaven man, with a face that looked like a common workman's, albeit with an unnaturally narrow forehead and minuscule eyes; he was wearing something between a jacket and a military tunic decked with medals, anchors and stars. The walls of the corridor were lined with several statues and busts of the same man. Finally we arrived—in complete silence—at a door, through which I was shoved into a room, where an elderly man in glasses was sitting at a large table. He was dressed in some peculiar semi-military, semi-civilian uniform, similar in style to the one depicted in the portraits and on the statues.

He began by extracting a massive revolver from a drawer and placing it beside a paperweight. Then, suddenly lifting his head and looking me straight in the eye, he said:

"Naturally you'll be aware that only a full and frank confession can save you?"

After the long walk down the corridor—the soldiers had walked briskly and I had been obliged to keep pace with them—I felt as if the almost semi-unconscious state in which I had until now found myself had at last given way to something more normal. My body once again felt as it usually did, I could see what was before my eyes with perfect clarity, and now it became more apparent to me than ever that what had happened was obviously the result of some misunderstanding. At the same time, however, the prison setting and the prospect of an arbitrary interrogation rather vexed me. I looked at the seated figure in glasses and asked:

"Forgive me, but who are you?"

"There'll be no questions here!" he answered sharply.

"There appears to be some confusion," I said. "I seem to recall hearing a distinctly interrogatory tone in your voice when you just addressed me."

"Try to understand that we're dealing with your life here," he said. "It's too late now for dialectics. Though perhaps it would be beneficial to remind you that you stand accused of high treason."

"High treason, no less?"

"No less indeed. You must have no illusions about it: it is a terrible charge. I repeat that only a full and frank confession can save you now."

"In what respect am I alleged to have committed high treason?"

"You have the impertinence to ask? Very well, I'll tell you. There is high treason in the very fact that you allow for the unlawful principle of there being any legitimacy in pseudo-governmental ideas that contradict the Great Theory of the Central State which has been devised by the foremost geniuses of mankind."

"What you're saying is so absurd and naive that I'm at a loss to respond. I would like only to point out that the possible admission of one principle or another is a theoretical stance, not a fact on the basis of which it's possible to prosecute a man."

"Even here, at a tribunal of the Central Government, you speak in a language whose every word echoes your crime. In the first instance, a representative of the state, particularly an investigator, is, as far as you're concerned, infallible, and no word of his may be termed either 'absurd' or 'naive'. But that's not all. Now, after what you've just said, there's another point that further compounds your guilt: causing insult to a representative of the Central Government. You stand accused of high treason, of conspiracy to assassinate the head of state and, finally, of the death of Citizen Ertel, one of our finest representatives beyond these borders."

"Who is this Ertel?"

"The man you killed. Don't try to deny it: nothing escapes the knowledge of the Central Government. A full confession is your only option; it is what the state and the people expect of you."

"The only response I'm able to give concerns Ertel. That man was a hired assassin. I was in a position of lawful self-defence. Evidently until now Ertel never had to deal with people in the habit of defending their own life, and this blunder wrought his downfall. As far as the remaining accusations are concerned, they're sheer nonsense, which speaks volumes for the intellectual capacity of the people who contrived them."

"You'll surely repent of those words."

"May I point out that the verb 'to repent' is inherently religious in its connotations? It seems strange to hear it on the lips of a representative of the Central Government."

"What will you say when confronted with your accomplices?"

I shrugged.

"Enough!" he said, firing the revolver: the bullet hit the wall about a metre and a half above my head. The door opened, and the soldiers who had brought me here entered the room.

"Take the accused to his cell," said the investigator.

As I was returning to my cell, glancing from time to time at the portraits and statues, only then did it occur to me that I had acted wrongly, that I should never have answered the investigator as I had done. I simply had to prove to him that there was no way I could be the man for whom he had mistaken me. Rather than adopt this tactic, however, I had spoken to him as though I admitted the absurd legitimacy of his argument, and in disagreeing with it, as it were, dialectically, I was playing straight into his hands. Besides, it was obvious that I was a complete stranger to this world in which I now found myself. The faces of the soldiers who escorted me had displayed a complete absence of thought or emotion. These portraits looked like oleographs produced by a workman whose lack of artistry unwittingly provoked both pity and scorn; likewise the statues. The investigator's words bore the mark of an equally grim intellectual poverty and, in the world I came from, any such man would have had no place in the machinery of justice.

Back in my cell, I was just about to tell my companion about the interrogation, when immediately I was led off again, this time in a different direction; I landed in front of a second investigator, who addressed me rather differently than the first had done.

"We are aware," he began, "that we are dealing with a relatively cultured man, and not just some mercenary from a hostile political organization. You must surely know that we are surrounded by enemies; this forces us to increase our vigilance and sometimes compels us to adopt measures that, although they may appear rather drastic, are not always avoidable. Such has been the case with you. We know, or at least we hope to establish, that your guilt is less severe than it may initially have seemed. Be candid with us; it is in your, and our, best interests."

Judging by the way he spoke, it was obvious that this man was much more dangerous than the first investigator. But I was almost glad of it; it was possible to talk to him in a different language.

"I can understand your frustration during the earlier interrogation," he continued. "There was a mistake, a most regrettable one: the investigator you spoke with usually handles only the simplest of cases, although he invariably strives towards matters clearly exceeding his competency. You see, he owes his position to party membership; one cannot make too many demands of him. Let us, however, get down to business. Are you aware of the charges brought against you?"

"I would like to know," I said, "who it is that I've been mistaken for. It's obvious to me that what has happened

39

here is the result of some misunderstanding, which I would very much like to clear up. My surname is"—I gave him my surname—"I live in Paris and I am a student of history at the university there. I have never—as is easy to ascertain through even the most superficial of investigations—engaged in any political activity, nor have I ever belonged to any political organization. The accusations concerning terrorist intentions are so absurd and illogical that I see no point in discussing them further. I admit that the man you take me for may be both a terrorist and your political adversary, but that has nothing to do with me. I only hope that your state apparatus is sufficiently organized to establish this."

"Are you alleging that Rosenblatt was mistaken? If so, your case will take a decidedly tragic turn."

"Who is this Rosenblatt? This is the first time I've heard the name, I've never seen the man."

"I must say, you did everything you could so that no one would ever see him again: you strangled him."

"Forgive me, but half an hour ago I was told that his surname was Ertel."

"That was a mistake."

"What, another mistake?"

"Personally speaking, I never much rated Rosenblatt," continued the investigator. "When you called him a hired assassin, you weren't far from the truth. The pity is that he was the only man who could have saved you. You've robbed him of the opportunity to do so. We have in our possession his secret report on you and your activities. The intelligence it contains is much too detailed and accurate to be a fabrication. And in any case, the man was utterly bereft of imagination."

"It's entirely possible that the intelligence contained in his report is accurate. But the single most important factor in all this is that it concerns someone else, and not me."

"Yes, but how are we to prove this?"

"For a start, this man cannot be my twin. Moreover, I presume he would have a different surname. Then, of course, there are other distinguishing features: age, height, hair colour, and so forth."

"Rosenblatt's report, although comprehensive in all other respects, unfortunately contains none of these indicators. And anyway, why should I believe you and not him?"

"You may not believe me. But there would be nothing easier than to make enquiries in Paris."

"We avoid, insofar as possible, all contact with foreign police."

It began to dawn on me that my situation was hopeless. The judicial machinery of the Central State displayed absolute rigidity and a lack of any interest in the accused; its function was solely punitive. The primitivism characteristic of all justice had been reduced to an absurdity. There was one single formula: anyone brought before the court stood accused of crimes against the state and was liable to be punished. The innocence of the accused was admissible theoretically, although it was bound to be disregarded. Obviously a hint of desperation glinted in my eyes, for the investigator said:

"I'm afraid you will find it objectively impossible to prove any error on our part. This leaves you with a choice: either to persist in this fruitless denial and thus knowingly to consign yourself to death, or else to sign a confession and make peace with the fact that you will spend a short period of time in prison, after which freedom awaits you."

"Do you hold the accused to be innocent until proven guilty?"

"Certainly."

"Then I cannot sign a confession for an act I haven't committed: doing so would result in my consciously perverting the course of justice in the Central State."

"Ideologically speaking, you're correct. But that isn't the point. You are obliged to act within the limitations of the options available to you. Unfortunately these are rather narrow, I'll grant you that. Let us enumerate them once again. On the one hand, a complete denial of guilt and the prospect of capital punishment. On the other, a confession and temporary deprivation of liberty. The rest is all theory. I advise you to think about this. I'll call for you again in the near future."

Back in my cell, I recounted the details of my first and second interrogations to my companion. He listened to me, sitting in that same pose with his eyes closed. When I finished, he said:

"That was easily foreseeable."

Again I looked upon his rags and his unshaven face and recalled that this man had promised my release.

"Do you think there's anything to be done about it?"

"You see," he began, disregarding my question, "I know these laws better than any investigator. They aren't actually laws, they're more the spirit of the system, not a statutory code of any sort."

He spoke as if he were giving a lecture.

"The absence of elementary legal norms is exacerbated by the fact that the ordinary workers of the judiciary are outstanding for a prodigious lack of culture and confuse their functions with those of some judicial executioner. You can crush their arguments and prove to them that twice two is four, that they are wrong and that the prosecution's case is based on naive folly, which is the case more often than not. But this simply doesn't register with them. They will still sentence you and adopt punitive measures—not because you're guilty and it has been proven, but because this is how they understand the task of the Central Judiciary. Objection is unfavourable and punishable in principle. To argue with the law is a crime against the state, as is to doubt its inerrancy. There are a dozen formulas, each of which expresses a particular type of ignorance; all the miscellaneous activities of millions of people can be condensed into these dozen formulas. To fight this system, which is difficult to define in a few words…"

"I would say: grim idiocy."

"Splendid. So, to fight this grim idiocy by rational means is impossible. One has to employ other strategies; which did you adopt when Ertel-Rosenblatt tried to strangle you?"

"Those that my sports instructors had taught me."

"Very well. Had you acted otherwise, you probably wouldn't have been long for this world."

"Quite possibly," I said, recalling the darkness, the fingers clutched at my neck, and how I had begun to choke.

"In this instance, knowing that neither your innocence nor your ability to prove it will achieve anything, you've got to change tack. I've discovered a way out; it's cost me dearly, but I have nothing left to fear now. My method is infallible, and that's why I assured you that you'd be freed. I repeat this promise to you now."

"I'm sorry, but if you have such a powerful weapon against this, then how is it that you've come to be in the same position as I am?"

"I already told you there's been a misunderstanding," he replied with a shrug. "They arrested me during the night, as I slept."

"What exactly is this weapon?"

He said nothing for a long time, although his lips moved silently, as they had done when I first saw him. Then, without raising his head, he said:

"I'm a hypnotist. It is I who dictates the findings to the investigator."

"And if he resists hypnosis?"

"I've yet to encounter such a case. But even if he were to resist this type of hypnosis, he would surely succumb to another."

"In other words…"

"In other words, I'd force him to end his life by committing suicide, and the matter would be reassigned to someone else who would be susceptible."

"One more thing," I said, astonished by his confidence. "I'll soon be summoned by the investigator, but you won't be present for the interrogation. Are you able to bend him to your will from a distance?"

"That would be significantly more difficult. But you and I shall be summoned almost simultaneously."

"How do you know that?"

"While you were being questioned by the first investigator, I was being questioned by the second."

Then this calm man sank into total silence, which he did not break during the course of those three days that passed as I awaited the next interrogation, at which—if I were to believe him—such incredible things were to occur. We were given food twice daily; at first I was unable to eat it, as it was so disgusting. Only on the third day did I manage to swallow a few spoonfuls of some clear-grey liquid and a crust of poorly baked bread that was revoltingly chewy. I felt weak, but my mind was alert. During all this time my cellmate did not touch his food. Mostly he remained absolutely still, and it was impossible to fathom how his muscles and joints could withstand such prolonged strain. Lying on my stone bed, I pondered how fantastical reality could be, and how there was a palpable sense of sheer inescapability in all my surroundings: the geometric composition of the walls and ceiling, opening onto a thirty-storey precipice where the sun and rain alternated, and the constant presence of this strange, ragged vagrant. Once, to break this stony silence, I started whistling an aria from *Carmen*, but the notes sounded so flat, so wild and so misplaced that I immediately stopped. I had time enough to contemplate many times over in minute detail what had happened to me and to establish that despite there being an undoubted logic to it, the combination of factors could but seem entirely irrational. Least of all did I think of the danger hanging over me, and in spite of the outward implausibility of what my companion had promised, I believed his every word.

Finally, on the evening of the third day, they came for me. I got up and for the first time in all this while felt a strange chill inside me, perhaps the remote fear of death, perhaps a deep-seated dread of the unknown. In any case, I knew that I was now powerless to defend myself. I thought how this made everything simpler and how I had faced less danger in that dark Parisian alley with the hands of an unknown assassin at my throat. Previously I had depended on myself for survival, on some primitive mental alertness and my natural agility. Now I was defenceless.

I was led into the investigator's office. He indicated a seat and offered me a cigarette. Then he asked:

"Have you thought about what I said to you during our last meeting?"

I nodded. The chill within me was for some reason preventing me from speaking.

"Will you sign your confession?"

I had to make an exceptional effort to reply to the investigator's question in the negative. I knew, however, that only the word "no" could possibly save me. I felt as if I lacked the strength to utter the word, and in that moment it dawned on me why people admit to crimes they have not committed. Every muscle in my body was tensed, the blood rushed to my face, and I felt as if I were bearing up an enormous weight. At last I replied:

"No."

Everything came crashing down before me, and I thought I was on the verge of losing consciousness. Yet I distinctly heard the investigator's voice:

"We've been able to ascertain that your testimony, while on first appearance most convincing—which will aggravate your guilt—was false. Your right-hand man in the organization you headed has betrayed you and signed a full confession."

I felt an immediate sense of relief. However, I had the impression that my voice lacked conviction.

"Neither the man, nor the organization you mention has ever existed. Your methods of prosecution are absurd."

At that moment the door opened and some soldiers brought my cellmate in. Then they withdrew. I quickly glanced at him; he instantly seemed to grow taller.

"Do you recognize this man?" asked the investigator.

"I do."

He obviously wanted to add something, but refrained from doing so. Silence ensued. The investigator got up from his chair and took a few steps about the room. Then he went over to the window and opened it. Next he returned, zigzagging, to his chair, but decided not to sit down, instead remaining standing in an unnatural and uncomfortable pose, half bent over. I sensed that something strange and troubling was happening to him.

"Are you feeling ill?" I asked.

He did not answer. The man in rags was staring at him intently, standing there without moving or saying a word.

The investigator again went over to the window and half leant out of it. Then, finally, he sat down at his desk again and began writing. Several times he tore up the sheets of paper and threw them into the waste-paper basket. This went on for some time. Beads of sweat formed on his face; his hands started shaking. Then he stood up and said in a strangled voice:

"Yes. I see that you've been the victim of some terrible mistake. *In accordance with your request*, I promise to undertake a thorough investigation of the matter and punish the guilty parties. On behalf of the Central Government, please accept my apologies. You are free to go."

He rang a bell. An officer in a blue tunic entered, and the investigator issued him with a pass. We left the room and delved once again into the endless passageways and corridors, whose walls were covered in those same paintings, lending the impression that we were walking past some military line-up of semi-officers, semi-civilians, great in number and all identical. Finally we reached an enormous gate, which silently swung open before us. Then I turned my head to speak to my companion and I nearly stopped dead in my tracks with amazement. Beside me was a tall, clean-shaven man in a handsome European suit; on his face he wore a sardonic smile. While the gates closed just as silently behind us, and before I could say a word, he waved goodbye to me, turned right and disappeared. Try as I might to look for him, I was unable to find him.

It was a sultry summer evening, the street lamps were lit, passing motor cars were sounding their horns, and

the traffic lights were flashing green and red at the cross-
ings. Savouring the joys of liberty, I fell to thinking about
what I might do in this foreign city where I knew no one
and had no place of refuge. But I continued walking.
The traffic began to quieten down. I crossed a narrow
river on a bridge flanked by impressive statues of water
nymphs; then I cut across some boulevard and started
walking up a street leading off at a slight angle. By now
it was perfectly quiet. I continued on for around two or
three hundred metres. At a turning leading onto a road
lined with single- and double-storey villas a dim street
lamp illuminated the metallic blue of a sign fixed to the
wall. I went up to it and with astonishing slowness made
out, as though emerging from deep slumber, blurred at
first, then gradually taking shape and becoming clearer
and clearer, white letters in the Latin alphabet looming
before my eyes. Instantly they became blurred again and
vanished, but a second later they reappeared. I extracted a
cigarette and lit it, burning my fingers on the match—and
only then did I comprehend the happy pattern of these
symbols. On a navy-blue plaque, in white lettering, was
written the words: 16ᵉ ARR-T, RUE MOLITOR.

I had long grown used to these attacks of mental illness.
Within what remained of my consciousness, in this small,
troubled space that at times almost ceased to exist, but
which nevertheless constituted my last hope of returning to the real world and not one darkened by chronic

madness, I tried stoically to endure these departures and excursions. Yet every time I returned I found myself in the grip of despair. The inability to overcome this inexplicable ailment was akin to being conscious of my own impending doom, of some moral handicap that set me apart from other people, as if I were unworthy of the popular happiness of being the same as everyone else. That evening, as I read those letters on the blue plaque, after a few moments of joy, I experienced something like the pain of a man who has just received confirmation of a terminal diagnosis. Paris that night seemed different than usual and unlike its true self; with a tragic finality the vista of street lamps illuminating the foliage on the trees served only to emphasize the incurable sorrow I felt. I thought about the future that lay ahead of me, the growing complexity of my existence, and my real life, which was difficult to discern among this mass of morbid, fantastical distortions that haunted me. I was unable to complete a single task that required any sustained effort or whose solution demanded an unbroken application of logic. Even in my personal relations there was always, or there always risked being, that element of mental derangement, which could strike at any moment and would distort everything. I could not be held wholly accountable for my actions, could never be certain of the reality of what was happening to me; I often found it difficult to distinguish what was real and what was a hallucination. And now, as I walked about

Paris, the city seemed no more real to me than the capital of the fantastical Central State. I had begun my latest journey in Paris, but where and when could I ever have witnessed anything like that imaginary labyrinth where the imperative momentum of my madness had driven me? The reality of that passageway, however, was borderline, and I remembered the turning and those strange recesses in the wall no less clearly than I did all the buildings in the street where I lived in the Latin Quarter. Of course, I knew for a fact that the street did exist, whereas the passageway had just been a product of my imagination; and yet this incontestable difference between the street and the passageway lacked the definite, concrete persuasiveness it ought to have held for me.

Now my thoughts turned elsewhere. Of all the districts in Paris, why had I wound up specifically in this one and not in another, not in Montmartre, for example, or in the Grands Boulevards? It was hardly likely to have happened by chance. I was unable to recall where I had headed as I left my apartment and what had induced me to undertake this journey. In any case, I had walked along, oblivious to both the buildings and the streets, as all this time I had been imprisoned in the Central State; nevertheless, I had set off in a particular direction and had apparently not lost my way, although it was clear that the part of my consciousness leading me there had functioned beyond any control of my own. There must have been an automatic precision, as happens when a man stops thinking about what he is doing and his actions take on a speed and accuracy that would be impossible were they to be directed by his consciousness. It was no coincidence that I had ended up here. But where could I have been going? A few years before I would often travel this route, because a woman with whom I had been very close lived nearby; back then I had known every building and every tree in the area. However, we parted a long time previously, and thereafter the streets leading to her apartment had shed their once thrilling aspect; their even vistas, at whose ends stood a building with an apartment on the fourth floor where my whole world—warm and transparent—had once been centred, now appeared unrecognizably foreign to me.

I couldn't remember, and I felt so weary that I decided to put an end to these fruitless endeavours and return home. Ultimately it did not really matter. I sat on the Métro for a long time, then I got off at Odéon and headed towards my hotel, spurred on by an irresistible urge—to lie down and sleep. By the time I finally found myself in bed, it was already night; I could hear the occasional footstep outside in the street, and from an invisible gramophone came the sound of a woman's voice singing '*Autrefois je riais de l'amour*'.* Soon I found myself sinking into a melancholy gloom, as starless and warm as the night itself,

* There was a time when I would laugh at love.

when suddenly, just as I was on the verge of slumber, I recalled that I had planned to pay a visit to Rue Molitor that evening, to the house of my acquaintance, the one who had so miraculously and so unexpectedly come into money.

* * *

I went to see him a few days later. This time neither his apartment nor the telephone on his writing desk, neither the books on the shelves nor the unusual tidiness that was in evidence everywhere, surprised me—firstly because I could never be any more surprised than I had been when I met him that day in the café, secondly because having lived for years in squalid hovels he should naturally be attracted to things of an opposite nature: instead of apocalyptic filth, cleanliness; instead of chaos, order; instead of a spit-spattered stone floor, gleaming parquet. In his general deportment, as in his every move, one sensed the convulsive tension of newfound gentility, which, on the face of it, seemed a little affected, at least to begin with.

When I arrived at his apartment—this would have been around four o'clock in the afternoon—he was not alone. A little man of around fifty, with indefinably grey hair and small, shifty eyes, was sitting in an expectantly servile pose, giving me to think once again how the term "plastique", so flaunted in arts and theatre reviews, was often cruelly and almost invariably inseparable from the circumstances of one's life, milieu and state of health, and how the word was so mutely expressive. He was very shabbily dressed and held in his hands a crumpled, soiled cap that had once been light grey—this was possible to discern from the light patches of fabric showing through at the peak, which had been protected by a button. As I entered, the man with the cap, who was in the middle of saying something, fell silent and shot me a look both angry and fearful. The host, however, stood up, greeted me—he was markedly courteous—apologized and said to his guest:

"Do go on, I'm listening. You say that it happened in Lyons?"

"Yes, yes, in Lyons. So, you see, after I was arrested…"

He told a rather convincing tale about how he had accidentally knocked down a pedestrian while riding a motorcycle, and how a long series of misfortunes had begun shortly thereafter. Judging from the way he spoke, fluently and with an astonishing lack of expression, as if the story did not concern him but some third party, to whose fate, incidentally, he was entirely ambivalent, it was clear that he had told this tale many times over and that even for him it had lost any degree of persuasiveness. I do not know whether he himself realized this. The crux of the matter was that following his release from prison his papers had been confiscated, and so now he was unable to take up any form of work, and thus found himself in a hopeless, as he phrased it, situation. The moment he uttered these words, I suddenly remembered having seen him once before and hearing those very words, whose intonation evidently never varied. I could even recall the whereabouts and the circumstances in which it had come about: it was near Gare Montparnasse, and his audience then had been a stout man with a beard—half merchant's, half pirate's—and the face to go with it: broad, boorish and pompous all at once. Following these words concerning the hopelessness of his situation, he paused and then said, turning away slightly and giving two half-hearted sobs, that if the gentleman did not help him, then the only thing left for him would be suicide. He added, waving his hand with casual desperation, that he had personally lost all his *joie de vivre*—he expressed it differently, but that was the sum of it—however, he pitied his wife, and it was possible that she would not survive the blow, for she was chronically ill and was not to blame. The mention of blame seemed rather peculiar to me, but he immediately explained that her second husband—he himself was her third—had given her syphilis, and now, he claimed, it was taking a toll on her health.

"Yes," mused the host, "indeed…"

Then he asked in an entirely different tone of voice:

"Who gave you my address?"

"I beg your pardon?"

"I asked, who gave you my address?"

"I… I'm sorry, I was just passing and thought that, perhaps, some Russians might live here…"

"In other words, you don't want to say. As you wish. Only I know that your surname is Kalinichenko, that you were arrested not in Lyons but in Paris, and not for knocking down a pedestrian but for theft."

The man in the cap became uncommonly agitated and, stuttering with rage, said that if the gentleman held such an unjust opinion of him then he had better take his leave. His humility having vanished, his little eyes took on a furious expression. He stood up and made a swift exit, without saying goodbye.

"Do you know him?" I enquired.

"Of course," he replied. "We all know one another more or less. That is, I mean to say, everyone who belongs, or belonged, to that milieu. Only he failed to suspect that the Pavel Alexandrovich Shcherbakov who lives in this apartment and whose address was given to him by Kostya Voronov, despite his assurances not to pass it on to another living soul, is none other than the same who formerly lived in Rue Simon le Franc. Otherwise, of course, he wouldn't have bothered with the story about Lyons and the motorcycle, which for thirty francs Chernov, the former writer, concocted and wrote down for him since he lacked the imagination with which to do it himself."

"So he made up the sick wife?"

"Not entirely," said Shcherbakov. "As far as I'm aware, my visitor has never been married. In such circles many legal formalities are deemed unnecessary. However, the woman he lives with is indeed syphilitic. But of course I wouldn't be able to tell you whether or not she's ever been married. I have my doubts. Let us agree that it's of little consequence either way. And now, after all that, permit me to say how happy I am to see you here."

The conversation immediately acquired a different, far more cultivated tone; as with everything else, there was a sense that Pavel Alexandrovich wished to forget the period preceding his current circumstances. Nevertheless, he started—he could not help but do so—with a comparison.

"For so long I was deprived," he began, "of entry to a world that had once been my own… perhaps because I'm no philosopher, and I'm certainly no stoic. I mean to say that for a philosopher, the external conditions of life—remember Aesop's example—should play no part whatsoever in the development of human thought. I must admit, however, that there are certain materialistic details at whose mercy a man can find himself—insects, filth, cold, foul odours…"

He was sitting in a deep armchair, smoking a cigarette, with a cup of coffee resting in front of him.

"…all this has a most unpleasant effect on a man. Perhaps it's some law of psychological mimicry gone too far. After all, it's quite understandable: we often know which conditions govern the inception of some biological law or other, but we cannot predict when that action will terminate, nor can we be sure that its effects will always be the same. Why is it that *King Lear* and *Don Quixote* should lose all meaning for me simply because I live in inadequately fine surroundings? And yet it is so."

I was only half listening to him. Before my eyes, doggedly returning to me, was that day in April two years ago when I first set eyes on him, standing there in his ornamental rags, with that dark, unshaven face. Now there were books in heavy leather bindings lined above his head, and the recherché elegance of his speech could in no way seem out of place.

I spent the whole evening with him and left, taking with me the memory of this unlikely metamorphosis, which was utterly baffling and seemed to contradict everything I had until now, consciously or unconsciously, considered plausible. This man had started off in the realm of fantasy and stepped into reality, and for me his existence contained all the luxurious absurdity of a Persian fairy tale, which troubled me.

Some time after this I again—completely by chance—bumped into the residents of Rue Simon le Franc. I ran into one of my former classmates, with whom I had long ago lost touch, but about whom I occasionally read in the newspapers, most often with regard to his latest arrest or conviction. He was an astonishing man, a chronic alcoholic who had spent his entire life in a drunken haze and had been spared from the grave only by virtue of an uncommonly strong constitution. When he first arrived in France, he worked in a number of factories, although this period did not last for very long: he started seeing some well-to-do girl, taking her to all the cabarets in town; then he caught her cheating on him, shot her new lover, was sent down and on his release began leading the most disparate of lives, one with which it was difficult to draw any comparison. He worked as a gardener in the south of France, journeyed to the Alsace, and had once been spotted in a village in the Pyrenees. For the most part, however, he lived in Paris, in the outlying slums, passing from one shady episode to the next, and, whenever he spoke of it, the narrative would always feature his being released on a lack of evidence and the clarification of some misunderstanding. Then again, it was utterly impossible to keep track of his tale; there was no way to distinguish where the inebriation ended and where the madness began. In any case, there could be no talk of any chronological sequence to what he said.

"You see, just as I get back from Switzerland, she starts telling me how this lady painter from Italy is planning to go off to Sicily, but just then—can you imagine!—a police inspector investigating that Greek journalist barges in, asking me what I was doing in Luxembourg a fortnight ago, while she claims that the doctor who treated the Englishman was the victim of some night-time attack—his head was smashed in, you see, he was terribly injured, and so he decided to go straight to the lady modeller who lives near the Porte d'Orléans."

He spoke as though each of his interlocutors was well informed about every individual he mentioned. However, I had never heard of any artists, Greek journalists or doctors, even from him, and I was not altogether sure that they really did exist, such as he described them. Amid the progressive atrophy of his mental faculties, or, rather, amid their incredible confusion, all conception of time vanished; he had no idea in which year we were living, and any semblance of continuity in his own existence appeared miraculously improbable. Thus he wandered about Paris in a drunken madness that had persisted for years, and it was astonishing that he ever found his way home or even recognized anyone. But he had grown much worse in recent years, was taken ill with consumption, and could not go on as he had done. I once met him in the street; he asked me for some money and I gave him what I had, but a few days later I received a note from him, saying that he was bedridden in his hotel room and had nothing to eat. I headed straight there.

He lived on the outskirts of the city, not far from the abattoirs. Nowhere had I seen more abject poverty. Below, a man with tattoos and the currish face of a criminal told me as he idly rinsed out cloudy glasses behind the bar that Michel lived at No. 34. Up and down the steep, narrow stairwell passed some rather suspect-looking people, and each floor bore the peculiar trace of some foul stench that seemed to permeate the entire building. Mishka was lying on the bed, unshaven, haggard and emaciated. By the head of the bed sat a woman of around sixty, clumsily trowelled in make-up and wearing a black dress and slippers. When I came in Mishka said to her in Russian:

"You may go now."

She stood up and, with hardly any expression in her voice, said, "Goodbye," her mouth agape, revealing a number of missing teeth, and left. I silently watched her go. Mishka asked:

"Don't you recognize her?"

"No."

"It's Zina."

"Which Zina?"

"You know, the famous one."

I had never heard of any famous Zina.

"What is she famous for?"

"An artist's sitter, a beauty. She was the lover of all the great artists. She was my lover, too, but now, you understand, all that's a thing of the past. Women no longer exist for me; I'd be too out of breath. It was just before I was in Versailles that I had some business with this Albanian architect who had an imbroglio with my little Swiss—"

"Wait, wait," I said. "Tell me a bit more about Zina."

"She's living with a marksman these days," said Mishka. He was entirely sober—probably for the first time in a long while. "The little swine, we had a run-in around five years ago; he almost stole the money I'd just received from this English girl, she'd just got married and—"

"Did he steal it or not?"

"Steal it he did, but he gave it back. I twisted his arm. Such a mousey little swine, you know. Well, of course she gave him syphilis. From what I gather he's always been a marksman, goes about telling some story involving a motorcycle, something about being arrested in Lyons. I say to him, 'What good is Lyons when I remember you in the prison at Versailles?' And prisons don't come any worse, upon my word of honour, the Santé's a thousand times better. God forbid you ever end up at Versailles, take this as a piece of friendly advice. It was Alexei Alexeyevich Chernov who wrote this chap's entire life story for him— that, my friend, is talent. I even have something of his, typed out."

And indeed he extracted from the shelf a dirty-grey notebook with very dog-eared corners and handed it to me. It was Chernov's novel *Before the Storm*. I read the opening lines:

"A winter dusk was falling over Petersburg, majestic as always. Pyotr Ivanovich Belokonnikov, a wealthy man of forty, belonging both by birth and by the education he received in the Page Corps to the high society of the

Palmyra of the North, was walking along the pavement, his fur coat undone. He had just taken leave of Betty, his mistress, and could not stop thinking about the marble white of her bosom and the burning caress of her sumptuous body."

I questioned Mishka about these people whom he knew so well. Despite the disjointedness of the narrative, I nevertheless managed to ascertain that Alexei Alexeyevich Chernov was that ill-looking, shabbily dressed old man whom I had seen many times and who would ask me for alms at the entrance to the Russian church. I also learnt that Zina had a daughter, Lida, who was around twenty-six years old and had at one time been married to some Frenchman; he had died suddenly, poisoning was suspected, and Lida encountered some unpleasantness. I had already had occasion to note that in Mishka's language the word "unpleasantness" more often than not denoted "prison". These days she sold flowers in the streets somewhere.

I returned to Mishka's hotel a few days later, but he was no longer there and no one could tell me what had happened to him. Only much later did I learn that he had died of consumption around a month after I last met him, in one of the sanatoriums just outside Paris. It was around the same time, while walking down Boulevard Garibaldi, that I once spotted a group of people coming towards me on the pavement. It was Zina and the mousey marksman, the one I had seen at Pavel Alexandrovich's on the day I paid him a visit, with a young woman, very shabbily dressed, with unkempt fair hair—Lida, just as Mishka had described her to me. They were all walking almost abreast of one another. Lida was lagging just a little behind. I could see a discarded cigarette lying in the middle of the pavement in front of them. As they approached it, the mousey man was clearly about to bend down, but at that moment, with a peculiar rhythmical precision and speed, Zina pushed his shoulder so hard that he very nearly fell over. Then, in one casual, precise movement, she picked up the cigarette end and in the same step continued onward. I was put in mind of the *dzhigits* who, while sliding down from their saddles, are able to pick up a kerchief lying on the ground as their horse races on at full gallop. I saw Lida smile, and could not help noticing that in her drawn, sickly face, despite its youthfulness, there was a definite, if somewhat alarming, attractiveness.

That evening when I ran into these people, with recent events still fresh in my memory—the visit to Shcherbakov, the conversation with Mishka, my impressions of the mousey marksman, Zina and her daughter—that evening a great distance had separated me from them, and all this ceased to occupy my mind. During the day I had felt strangely exhausted; I had come home and slept for three whole hours. Then I got up, washed and went out to dine at a restaurant, but from the restaurant I went straight home again. It was around nine o'clock in the evening. I stood for a long time by the window, looking down onto the narrow street. Everything was as it always was: the stained glass of the brothel opposite my apartment was lit up and above it one could easily read the sign *"Au panier fleuri"*;* the concierges sat on their stools, in front of their doors, and amid the evening silence I could hear their voices conversing about the weather and the high cost of living; at the corner, where the street met the boulevard, Mado's silhouette kept appearing and disappearing by the windows of a bookshop as she went about her work, back and forth along that same stretch—thirty paces there, thirty paces back; somewhere nearby a pianola was playing. I knew everyone on this street, just as I knew every odour, the look of every building, the glass of every window pane, and that lamentable imitation of life, intrinsic to each of its inhabitants, which never revealed its greatest secret: what inspired these people in the lives they led? What were their hopes, their desires, their aspirations, and to what end did each of them obediently, patiently repeat the same thing day after day? What could there be in all this—apart from some biological law that they obeyed unknowingly and unthinkingly? What had summoned them to life out of apocalyptic nothingness? The accidental and perhaps momentary union of two human bodies one evening or late one night a few dozen years ago? And so I recalled

* The Flower Basket.

what Paul, a short, stout forty-year-old man in a cap, who
worked as a lorry driver and lived two floors below me,
had said over a glass of red wine:

"*J'ai pas connu mes parents, c'est à s'demander s'ils ont jamais
existé. Tel, que vous m'voyez, j'ai été trouvé dans une poubelle, au
24 de la rue Caulaincourt. Je suis un vrai parisien, moi.*"*

And when I once asked Mado what she planned to do
in the future and how she expected her life to turn out,
she looked at me with heavily pencilled empty eyes and,
shrugging her shoulders, replied that she never wasted
any time thinking about such things. Then she paused for
a second and said that she would work until the day she
died—"*jusqu'au jour où je vais crever, parce que je suis poitrinaire.*"†

I withdrew from the window. The pianola mercilessly
went on playing one aria after the next. I felt as if I were
venturing deeper and deeper into some vague mental fog.
I tried to envisage everything my mind could envelop in
the most comprehensive terms possible—the world as it
was right now: the dark sky above Paris, its enormous
expanse, thousands upon thousands of kilometres of
ocean, the dawn over Melbourne, late evening in Moscow,
the rushing of sea foam along the shores of Greece,
the midday heat in the Bay of Bengal, the diaphanous
movement of air across the earth, and time's unstoppable

* I never knew my parents, that is, if they ever existed at all. You
wouldn't think it to look at me, but I was found in a bin, at 24 Rue
Caulaincourt. I'm a real Parisian, I am.

† ...until the day I croak, because I'm consumptive.

march into the past. How many people had died while I had been standing there by the window, how many were now in their last agony as I had this very thought, how many bodies were writhing about in the throes of death—those for whom the inexorable final day of their lives had already dawned? I closed my eyes and before me appeared Michelangelo's *Last Judgement*, and for whatever reason I immediately recalled his final epistle, in which he stated that he could write no more. As I remembered these lines I felt a chill run down my spine: this hand that was now incapable of writing had carved *David* and *Moses* from marble—and yet his genius was dissolving into that very same nothingness from which it had come; each of his works was an apparent victory over death and time. So that these concepts—time and death—appeared to me in all their finality, I had to tread the long path of gradual immersion, and conquer the aural inadequacy of this series of letters, "t", "m", "d", "h", and only then did the infinite perspective of my own journey towards death come into view. Those lines in Michelangelo's letter rang in my ears, and I saw the printed page plainly before my eyes: the date, "Rome, 28 December 1563", and the address, "Lionardo di Buonarroto Simoni, Florence". "I have received many letters from thee of late to which I have not replied because my hand no longer submits to my will." Two months later, in February 1564, he died. Did he still recall the tragic grandeur of that swell of muscles and bodies that his relentless inspiration had so imperiously cast down into hell—with the countless, unerring movements of that truly unique hand, the very one that would later refuse to serve him—in the days when the illusion of his superhuman might and the earthly vanity of his singular genius became so apparent? I sat in my armchair and with cold rage pondered the fundamental bankruptcy of everything, in particular any abstract morality and even the unattainable spiritual loftiness of Christianity—because of the limitations imposed on us by time, and because of the existence of death. Of course, none of these thoughts were revelatory; I had known them my whole life, just as millions of others had known them before me, but only rarely did they cross from a theoretical understanding into something tangible, and whenever they made this transition I experienced a peculiar and incomparable terror. My entire world and everything that surrounded me would lose all meaning and sense of reality. Later I developed a strange and abiding desire—to vanish into thin air, like a phantom in a dream, like a patch of morning mist, like someone's distant memory. I wanted to forget everything, everything that constituted me, beyond which it seemed impossible to imagine my own existence, this aggregate of absurd, random conventions—as though I desired to prove to myself that I had not one life, but many, and consequently that the conditions in which I found myself in no way limited my options. I observed, from a theoretical and conceptual standpoint, the whole sequence of my gradual metamorphoses, and among the multitude of images to appear before me was the hope of some illusory immortality. I saw myself as a composer, a miner, an officer, a labourer, a diplomat, a tramp: there was something convincing about each transformation, and so I began to believe that I really had no idea who I might be the very next day or what distance would separate me from this night after the darkness had passed. Where would I be and what awaited me? I had lived what seemed like so many different lives, so often had I shuddered as I experienced the suffering of another, so often had I acutely felt what affected other people, often the dead or those far away from me, that I had long lost all concept of my own profiles. So on that evening, as happened whenever I was left alone for a lengthy period of time, I found myself surrounded by this sensual ocean of innumerable memories, thoughts, experiences and hopes, which were both preceded and succeeded by a vague and overwhelming sense of expectation. Ultimately I would be so wearied by this state of being that everything would begin to get mixed up in my imagination, and then I would either go out to a café or else try to concentrate on a single, specific idea or series of ideas, or perhaps I might try to rack my memory for some salutary melody that I would force myself to follow through to its end. As I lay in my bed in a state of total debility, I suddenly recalled the Unfinished Symphony; it resonated in the evening silence of my room, and after several minutes I began to feel as if I were once again in a concert hall: the black tail-coat of the conductor, the intricate floating dance of his baton, whose movements amid the vanquished silence led the music—strings, bows, piano keys—the immediate and essentially miraculous return of distant inspiration, halted many years ago by that blind and merciless law, the same law that stayed Michelangelo's hand. Night was setting in and there were already stars in the sky, downstairs the concierges were asleep, the sign *"Au panier fleuri"* was shining brightly, and at the corner, like a pendulum, Mado was pacing back and forth—and all this filtered through the Unfinished Symphony, without darkening it or disturbing it, gradually blurring and disappearing in this whirl of sound, in this illusory victory of memory and imagination over reality and perception.

* * *

I visited Pavel Alexandrovich almost every week and talked at length with him. I wanted to understand exactly how he had been reduced to the position in which I had found him when we first met, and how, once in this position, he had managed to preserve what had so sharply distinguished him from his comrades in misfortune. I knew that when a man becomes impoverished the road back is almost always inaccessible, not only in terms of a return to material well-being—many poor people were comparatively wealthy in my experience—but mainly in what is termed social stratification: they did not, as a rule, rise up from their newfound status. Naturally, I never posed this question directly, nor did I even allude to it. However, reading between the lines of a few off-hand remarks made by Pavel Alexandrovich, I was able to construct a plausible narrative. Something had happened during his early years abroad—I never learnt what exactly—a tragedy linked to some woman, it seemed. Thereafter he had taken to drink. Thus his situation had continued for a number of years and probably nothing would have saved him had it not been for the fact that he fell ill. One night he collapsed in the street and lay there for several hours, until he was picked up and taken to a hospital. There he was given a thorough examination, all the necessary tests were carried out, he underwent treatment for several months, and when at last he felt sufficiently recovered the doctor told him that he would survive only on the provision that he completely abstained from alcohol. Pavel Alexandrovich was soon enough convinced of the truth in the doctor's words: a single glass of wine immediately induced vomiting and excruciating pain. He gave up drinking and after a short while regained the majority of his health. By the time we met in the Jardin du Luxembourg, he had already been teetotal for a year and a half. He had long already felt the acute shame of his situation, but now he was old, physically frail, and for many years had led the life that his former acquaintances were now leading, and he fancied that if nothing were to change in the near future, there would be only one thing for it—suicide.

Such was the apparent explanation for what had happened to him. It seemed to me, however, that there must have been something else—the constant passive resistance of his unquestionable innate culture to that sudden fall, some internal, perhaps almost subconscious, almost organic stoicism, which he himself so stubbornly denied.

Naturally, I couldn't help but notice that there was a woman living in his apartment, although I had never once set eyes on her, and Pavel Alexandrovich never so much as said a word about it. However, I often spotted evidence of her presence: in the ashtray lay cigarette ends bearing the imprint of encrimsoned lips, and a barely perceptible hint of perfume would linger in the room. But what ultimately could have been more natural? And so one day when I arrived—as usual, towards eight o'clock in the evening—I found not two, but three place settings at the table.

"There will be three of us for dinner this evening," said Pavel Alexandrovich, "assuming you've no objection."

"On the contrary," I hastened to say. That very moment I heard footsteps and turned my head—I started with surprise and an unexpected feeling overwhelmed me: before me stood a young woman, in whom I instantly recognized

Zina's daughter, although she was completely transformed since that day I saw her on the street with her mother and the mousey marksman. She was elegantly attired in a navy-blue silk dress, fairly broad with ample pleats; her fair hair was combed in waves, her lips were crimson, and her eyes lightly pencilled. But still there was that same look about her face that I had spotted when I first set eyes on her and which was extremely difficult to define—something both attractive and unpleasant at the same time.

She offered me her hand and excused herself, saying that she often found it difficult to express herself in Russian. She pronounced her "r"s as the French do and continually lapsed into French during the conversation—but there she had nowhere to hide. She spoke much as people did on the streets in the poorer quarters of Paris, and I shuddered to hear these familiar intonations, that itinerant mass of sounds, wretched and somehow genuinely tragic. In any case, she remained mostly silent, occasionally transferring her gaze from Shcherbakov to me and back again, irking me somewhat with her absurd air of self-importance. She was twenty-six years old, although to look at she seemed older, as her complexion had lost the taut freshness of youth, and because there was a slight hoarseness in her voice when she lowered it. But even this held a peculiar allure…

That evening I knew almost nothing about her. I could have learnt everything from Mishka, but he was no longer among the living. I had, however, alternative sources of information, of which I later availed myself: I invited one of the Russian tramps I knew by sight to accompany me to a café, and on the third glass of wine he revealed a lot about her life to me. But this happened five or six days after our dinner for three.

Pavel Alexandrovich, as always, did not touch the wine; I took a few sips. Lida, on the other hand, drank four glasses. After dinner Pavel Alexandrovich asked me whether I liked Gypsy romances. I replied that I did.

"Then let me invite you to a little amateur concert," he said.

We retired to the other half of the apartment, which until then I had not had the opportunity of seeing. There was a fur rug on the floor, and the walls were decorated in dark-blue wallpaper. In the drawing room there was a piano. Pavel Alexandrovich seated himself at it, lightly stroked the keys and said:

"Shall we, Lida?…"

She began sotto voce, although it was immediately clear that she was musically gifted, that she was incapable of hitting a wrong note or missing a beat. After a minute she seemed to forget about us and began singing as if she were alone in the room—alone, or in front of a full auditorium. I was familiar with almost all her repertoire, as extensive as it was, which included French *chansons*, Gypsy romances and many other songs of the most varied and random origins. But until this evening I had never imagined that they could sound like this. To her performance, which could in no way be criticized in terms of its artistry or its musical sincerity, she brought a sustained, grave sensitivity, so often lacking in these works. In her voice, now lingering, now brief, now deep, in all its various timbres, there was always that same unrelenting insistency, which ended up overwhelming the piano, the singing, the sequence of rhyming words, until it became simply painful. There was an inexplicable auditory wantonness about it, and as I closed my eyes the white gulf of an imaginary bed appeared before me, and in it was Lida's naked body with the vague silhouette of a man bending over her. However, the most unpleasant thing about it all was a sort of personal reminder—a reminder that no one in her audience was or could be entirely indifferent to this suffocating sensual world. And so even then, as I listened to her singing, I knew that perhaps all it would take to draw me irresistibly towards her was one random twist of fate, and neither my instinctual contempt for her nor the chronic psychological illness that kept dragging me into that cold abstract space from which there was no escape would be able to fight off this allure. As these thoughts went about in my mind, I suddenly felt infinitely sorry for Pavel Alexandrovich; one could only assume that in that world of which she was an irresistible living reminder he had been assigned the pitiful role of her insipid companion—just as he could only be her accompanist in this auditory union of piano and voice. I paid close attention to Lida—to her red mouth, to her eyes, which occasionally took on a dreamy, misty expression, to the rhythmic swaying of her slender body, which accompanied her singing.

> *A ray of sunlight passes through the bolted shutter,*
> *Again my head, like yesterday, begins to spin,*
> *I hear your laughter and our recent conversation,*
> *Your words ring out just like the sound of plucking strings.*

Suddenly I remembered her mother, Zina, with her aged, clumsily painted face, her toothless mouth and lifeless eyes, and her rheumatic feet in evening slippers. Then I returned my gaze to Lida; her features blurred and receded into the distance, and then, feeling a sudden chill run down my spine, I momentarily glimpsed the vanished similarity between Lida and her mother. Lida, however, had far to go before she would reach this stage—I could but muse how many times over, in the course of the long years ahead, Lida's body would move in that swaying rhythm and how someone else's eyes would look at her with the same avid attention with which I was watching her now. By the time she had finished singing I felt drunk; I left almost immediately, alluding to a need to prepare for an exam, and only outside did I once again feel free.

A few days later I sought out a former acquaintance of mine, an old Russian marksman, someone I would have recognized even from afar, because it was impossible to mistake him for anyone else: his facial hair grew in patchy, isolated clumps. Two or three times I had seen him cleanly shaven, and only then did he begin to resemble other people. But when he was unshaven, which was most of the time, there was something almost botanical, something resembling patches of grey moss forcing their way through rock, about this strange growth on his face. I invited him into a small café, ordered him a glass of red wine and a sandwich—he ate very little, like all alcoholics—and asked him whether he knew Zina, her husband and her daughter. At first he answered evasively, but soon enough the wine set to work on him, and he told me everything he knew about what he called "that family". I had to make a tremendous effort, however, to get him to talk about what interested me, as he would constantly digress onto a never-ending tale of some princess, a former mistress of his, whom he swore he would never forget and who had made such a wonderful career for herself in Paris, which, incidentally, was only to be expected, as she was such an exceptional woman. I couldn't quite gather what sort of career it was exactly, all the more so as my friend said that it had taken years of patience and careful planning for the princess to achieve her aims. In the event, it all became clear: the princess, it turned out, had worked as a lady's maid for an old woman who was almost deaf and blind, and whom she had systematically robbed. And when the old woman died, leaving her fortune to some distant relatives, the princess found herself in possession of a considerable sum of money. It was then, he said, that she scorned his love and retreated into herself. He was clearly looking to me for sympathy; I nodded and vaguely remarked that these things happen and that fortune is not always the privilege of the worthy. He shook my hand with drunken sincerity and at last began on Zina and Lida. He related to me their story with such details that seemingly no one could have known, yet he mentioned them as if they were plain for all to see. First, he alleged that Zina herself did not know who Lida's father was, because she had led a rather varied life in those days. Until the age of twelve, Lida had lived in the countryside, and only then did she come to live with her mother. At fourteen, she became the lover of the mousey marksman; when Zina found out about this there was a terrible scandal, she launched herself at her the man and wounded him with a pair of scissors—"In a fit of female jealousy," said the marksman. Later, however, everything "returned to normal", particularly after Lida ran away from home and disappeared for four years. Precisely how she spent them, no one, not even my informant, knew. True, one of his friends, Petya Tarasov, said that he had seen Lida in Tunis, selling things along the waterfront, but it was impossible to believe everything that Petya Tarasov said, since he was a drunkard, and the marksman also spoke disapprovingly of him, averring that he was an untrustworthy man. It subsequently came out, however, that Lida had indeed lived in Tunis. Then she returned home; her appearance had given one to suspect that she had been ill for a long time.

"Did they all live on Rue Simon le Franc back then?" I enquired.

No, it turned out that they had never lived there: they had an apartment in Rue de l'Église Saint-Martin.

"An apartment?" I said in astonishment. I knew this street; it didn't seem at all possible for there to have been any apartments there—there were only wooden huts housing Polish labourers, Arabs and Chinese, and on the corner was Bar Polski, one of the most sinister places I had ever seen. According to the description provided by my friend, however, Zina's apartment consisted entirely of two rooms, with no running water, gas or even electricity. I felt it would be too much to ask where Zina got the money for her meagre living; I knew that such questions were inappropriate among this sort of people. But the marksman explained to me that Zina and Lida earned decent money going from one building to the next, singing, while the mousey marksman accompanied them on the accordion. This had gone on until Zina somehow managed to ruin her voice for good. The money they earned did not last either, as Zina drank and the marksman gambled at the races—and so he lost what Zina did not manage to drink. It was impossible to rely on Lida, as she stayed at home infrequently and had not long ago married a young Frenchman, whose parents had disowned him and who died soon thereafter, injecting himself with an overdose of morphine, following which Lida was arrested, but released a few days later. Then my acquaintance informed me that Lida was now living with Pasha Shcherbakov, about whom he also spoke in considerable detail, and what he said largely tallied with what I already knew. I could but marvel at how remarkably well informed this man was. He knew the life story of the mousey marksman, too, as well as the unfortunate incident with the motorcycle, which had been fabricated by Chernov, with whom he was also familiar. Regarding the mousey marksman, he said that back in Russia he had been an accountant, in Astrakhan, or maybe it was Arkhangelsk, who since the outbreak of war had served in the commissariat, and later arrived abroad with a certain amount of money, although he was soon ruined, losing most of it at Monte Carlo and the remainder at the races. He had even met Zina at a racecourse, the Auteuil, on that fateful day when he bet practically everything he had on the famous, incomparable Pharaoh III, the finest horse ever to race in France. The jockey, however, had been bribed by a jealous rival and, leading Pharaoh with "the stick", threw the race at the finish line, so that no one would be any the wiser. As he told me this, my acquaintance showed clear signs of excitement. Moreover, he had displayed such a knowledge of racing terminology as to leave me in no doubt regarding his expertise in this area—and so I fell to thinking that the causes leading people to Rue Simon le Franc were really rather few, and almost never varied. "It was in losing my fortune that I gained Zina," the mousey marksman was reputed to have said in the days after the incident.

"That was probably another of Chernov's inventions," I said without holding back.

Thereupon we parted, and my companion left, expressing the hope that everything he had said would remain between the two of us. The phrase seemed unnecessary and automatic, devoid of all meaning, if for no other reason than the fact that he had said at the beginning of our conversation that the events he described were "known to everyone". Naturally, I did not number among the ranks of this "everyone", and there was something illicit and perhaps even vaguely hostile about my interest in this world. In any case, so it may have appeared to him. It was understandable to a degree, and were I in his shoes, I too, most likely, would have marked the brazenness and the impertinence of the fact that a well-heeled young man should suddenly intrude in an area that was divorced from him by this series of irrevocable falls—horses, alcohol, morphine, jail, syphilis, beggary—feeble depravity and filth, illness and physical frailty, the daily prospect of death on the street, and the total absence of hope, or even the slightest illusion of attaining anything better. I think this is what he meant when he uttered that phrase, saying that our conversation would remain between the two of us. But he had no way of knowing, of course, that despite the difference in outward appearances my position was, perhaps, no less pitiful, albeit in a different way, than his.

No one, not a single person in the entire world, apart from Catherine, knew that I was afflicted by this strange mental illness, the presence of which would so invariably depress me. Particularly excruciating was the consciousness of my own inequality and other people's superiority over me. I knew that at any moment I could lose all grip of reality and be plunged into an excruciating delirium, stripped of my defences for its duration. Luckily, I would usually sense the onset of such an attack, but sometimes it would come on all of a sudden and, terrified, I would ponder what might happen, in the library, on the street or during an exam. I did everything I could to escape it: I played a great deal of sport, every morning I would take a cold shower, and I am able to say that, physically speaking, I was in perfect health. But it was of no use. Perhaps, I thought to myself, if I were to survive an earthquake or being shipwrecked on the open sea or some other unimaginable, almost cosmic catastrophe, perhaps then there would be a turning point, a jolt that would allow me to take that first, most difficult step on the journey back to reality,

GAITO GAZDANOV

which I had so vainly sought all this time. But nothing of the sort happened, nor did it seem possible that it would happen, at least in the near future.

I continued to visit Pavel Alexandrovich, and were it not for my ongoing wariness of Lida's presence—although she seldom joined us—I might have said that it was only there that I found true spiritual repose. There was something pleasantly hypnotic about the serene comfort of the life that Pavel Alexandrovich now led, and this could be felt everywhere, beginning with the warm intonations of his voice and ending with the astonishing softness of his armchairs. Even his meals seemed to contain that very essence: nowhere before had I eaten such velvety soup, such cutlets, such crèmes au chocolat. I was so sincerely well disposed towards him that it pained me to think something bad might happen to him. This thought would probably never have tormented me, had I been able to forget about Lida. Naturally, I never allowed myself to ask Pavel Alexandrovich about this aspect of his life; he in turn never mentioned it. One evening, however, during one of my regular visits, he said to me—this was on a Friday—that the next day, on Saturday, he would be leaving Paris. He wanted to rent a gîte near Fontainebleau for the summer and planned to go there so that he would have ample time to survey the surrounding areas, to go for a stroll in the woods and to decide whether it was worth decamping there for the summer months.

"I haven't been to the woods for years," he said. "But I've never forgotten the feeling I would always get whenever I went there—a sense of the ephemerality of everything. You only have to look at a tree that's a few hundred years old to grasp the fleetingness of your own existence. I'll tell you what I think of it once I'm back. Lida will be staying on in Paris by herself. You will invite her to the cinema, won't you?"

"Yes, certainly, with pleasure," I said. That instant I began thinking how I would later cite a lack of time and do everything within my power to avoid this.

The following evening, however, I began to feel that it would simply be discourteous on my part to break a promise I had made to Pavel Alexandrovich. I vaguely told myself that this rationalization was as artificial as it was unfounded. Refusing to dwell on the thought, however, I telephoned Lida. She said she would be expecting me. I went to pick her up after dinner; by the time I arrived she was ready, and so we set off for the cinema.

I distinctly remember the film we saw, as well as the name of the actor starring in the lead role and his many adventures. This was all the more surprising, given that only a few minutes after the lights went down I accidentally brushed Lida's burning arm and everything began to blur. I knew that something irreparable was happening, but I was unable to stop myself. I placed my arm around her right shoulder, which in a soft and pliant motion drew nearer to me, and from that moment on I lost all control of myself. As we exited the cinema and turned down the first street—I was unable to speak from excitement and she, too, uttered not a single word—I held her waist to me, her lips approached my mouth, I felt the touch of her body beneath her light dress and sensed something like a moist burning. Right above my head a signboard for a hotel was illuminated. We went in and followed the maid upstairs, who was for some reason wearing black stockings.

"Number nine," a man's voice called from below.

Above the bed a large rectangular mirror was fixed to the wall, opposite the bed stood a mirrored screen and farther on there was a mirrored wardrobe; a few moments later, all these glaring surfaces began reflecting our bodies. There was something apocalyptic and blasphemous in this fantastical multiplicity of reflections, and I started to think about the Book of Revelation.

"*On dirait de la partouze,*"* said Lida.

She had a hot, dry body, and the burning sensation never left me. I knew I would never forget these hours. I began to lose myself in the unexpected richness of physical sensations, and there was something almost merciless about the perpetual allure of her body. The words she uttered through those firmly clenched teeth seemed remarkably strange—as if there were no space for them amid the torrid heat of the room, they sounded like

* It looks like an orgy.

a futile reminder of something that no longer existed. I now found myself in another world, which, naturally, I had never known before, in all its feminine irresistibility. This was what she had sung of that evening as I had listened to her! How faintly now the accompaniment of the piano sounded in my memory—a scarcely audible musical prattling. Fragments of thought flashed through my mind. No, I had never imagined that I could find myself wholly consumed by physical passion, so utterly that it left almost no room for anything else. I stared fixedly beneath me, at Lida's ecstatic face, at her wide, half-open lips that somehow reminded me of the cruel lines at the mouth of some stone goddess I had once seen—but had forgotten where and when. As before, a great many hands, shoulders, hips and legs were writhing about in the mirrors, and I began to suffocate from this impression of multiplicity.

"My darling," Lida began in a monotone voice. It seemed as if these sounds were having difficulty forcing their way through the thick sensual mist. "I've never loved anyone as I love you."

She was now lying next to me, exhausted and spent from the sustained exertion. But gradually her voice became deeper and clearer.

"*Je n'ai pas eu de chance dans ma vie*,"* she went on. "I lost my innocence at fourteen."

* I haven't had much luck in life.

She continually switched from French to Russian and from Russian back to French.

"Haven't you seen my mother's lover? He was old even then. He's limp, like a rag; he's no man. It hurt me and it was so dull, I wanted to cry because of how disgusting it all was. *Est-ce que tu me comprends? Dis-moi que tu me comprends.*"*

I nodded. She lay there naked—beside me, above me, beneath me—reflected in the still lustre of the mirrors. Again I had the impression—as so often happened—that a pair of eyes was staring at me fixedly from those terrible glass depths, and with cold despair I recognized the gaze as my own.

It required an extraordinary effort to overcome the sense of revulsion I now felt towards Lida and myself. I was, however, less inclined to blame her than I was to blame myself. In my conduct there had been an element of such flagrant baseness, of which I had until now not believed myself capable. Henceforth, who could tell what I might do and what other degradation awaited me? Everything inside me that I considered vaguely positive had been swept away by one chance encounter, but at what cost? I was consumed by other, more immediate considerations. I thought that if the matter had concerned only me, no one—least of all Pavel Alexandrovich—would have found out about this evening with Lida. But I couldn't be sure of her. She might tell the story to her next lover; she

* Do you understand me? Tell me that you understand me.

might ultimately confess to Pavel Alexandrovich, and that would place me in a hopeless position. How could I make this disappear, and what wouldn't I give for the chance to regain what there had been at the beginning of the evening? I thought about this as I lay next to her. I closed my eyes so as not to see her, and in front of me appeared that gentle mist, the same one that I had emerged from and returned to so often before, crossing from one world into another and finding myself once again in this noiseless abyss, after every psychological catastrophe. I sank into the familiar silence, so empty and dead that even the echo of this current misfortune was muted, because nothing mattered any more. Still, however, growing ever more dim, a light flickered before me; somewhere in the distance the last muffled sounds to reach me were dying away. And next to me, in this silent arena, lay Lida's naked body, as still as a corpse.

"*Monsieur, la séance est terminée,*"* said a far-off woman's voice.

Then it drew closer and repeated:

"*La séance est terminée, monsieur.*"

I opened my eyes. I was sitting in an empty cinema theatre; the curtain had already been drawn across the canvas of the lifeless screen. The usherette who had pronounced these words was looking at me with a mixture of surprise and sympathy.

* Sir, the show is over.

"Excusez-moi," I said. *"Merci de m'avoir réveillé, mademoiselle."**

I left the cinema. There were stars in the sky, and the night was warm and peaceful. I could see stone buildings with their bolted iron shutters, tranquil street corners, the brightly illuminated windows of the cafés. And for the first time ever, my return to reality appeared to lack the sad numbness that usually accompanied it; instead there was something almost buoyant about it. I imagined that willpower would triumph one day over my illness and everything that had haunted me so relentlessly would disappear not for a period of time, but for ever. Then, of course, my real life would begin. Later, whenever those visions returned to me—those to do with the imaginary meeting with Lida, the hotel and the mirrors—I would try to think about something else at once, although I knew I could never deceive myself: what I found disgusting had, in effect, really happened, and if it were not vested in the concrete form of accomplished fact, then this was merely an arbitrary, meaningless detail. It was precisely this absence of fact, however, that offered me an unassailable argument, an indisputable justification—and on that evening this deceptive piece of evidence seemed like a happy solution to the problem.

* * *

* My apologies… Thank you for waking me up, mademoiselle.

Some time after this episode I turned once again to my informant, who was not difficult to track down: by day he could be found in a café near Place Maubert, where the fag-end men congregated; by night one would have to journey to Montparnasse. In his endless pilgrimages across Paris there were places where this man would always go, much as others would go to their clubs. After a second glass of wine, he was ready to tell me everything I required—what he knew, what he had heard, and even what he did not know but was the object of his speculation. Of course, whatever we spoke of, he would always begin with one and the same thing—his princess, whose betrayal he could never forgive.

"While we're sitting here talking," he said, wiping his lips with the little finger of his right hand, not without a certain degree of coquettishness, "that bitch is lounging about in satin sheets in her apartment. But she doesn't realize that I've got her right where I want her."

"How so?"

"My good man, all I need to do is to go to the right place and say to the relevant person: '*Monsieur, vous savez l'origine d'sa richesse?*'"*

His French was fluent, although he overemphasized all his nasals and pronounced the French "o" like a Russian "a".

His faded, drunken eyes stared right at me.

"Only she suspects, of course, that Kostya Voronov has always been a *gentleman*"—this word he pronounced

* Sir, d'you know where her wealth came from?

91

entirely after his own fashion—"and that he would be entirely incapable of doing such a thing. Do you know what my nickname is?"

I replied that I hadn't the faintest idea.

"'The Gentleman'," he said. "That's what they call me. Here he is, standing before you—Kostya Voronov, gentleman, lieutenant of the Imperial Army. As I recall, the dispatch read: 'Distinguished himself through unflinching bravery, setting an example to his commanding officers and subordinates alike…' That's the sort of man she's betrayed. And why? Because, my dear fellow, Kostya Voronov had no intention of compromising himself, that's why."

I failed to understand exactly what he meant by this and how he might have compromised himself with the princess, but I did not press the matter, fearing too involved an explanation. He looked at me, clearly searching for some sympathy, as he always did when the conversation touched upon his personal life. I again uttered some words about the vicissitudes of fate.

"Fate, you know, is nothing but what meets the eye," he said. "Take, for instance, a man who lives life in the belief that everything is just splendid, whereas in actual fact, you see, he's living in a fool's paradise."

I asked the Gentleman whether this assertion was to be taken as a purely philosophical conceit, or whether it might contain any specific allusion.

"Both," he replied. "On the one hand, it holds true in general terms; on the other, take Pashka Shcherbakov, for example. I've nothing against him. Good God, I've known him for such a long time. He's not a bad sort; he's a clever chap, one of ours."

I shot a glance at him. He was standing in front of me, grim and unshaven, wearing a soiled, tattered jacket and an alarmingly narrow pair of trousers full of holes; a yellow cigarette was drooping from his lip, smoking.

"He lives like a lord now—good nosh, of course, an apartment and a girl, just as you'd expect."

He shook his head and drank up the remainder of his wine. I called the waiter and ordered another glass for him.

"I like it when people take a hint," said the Gentleman. "We are Russians, after all. But to get back to Pashka. That girl of his can barely stand him, because she's in love with Amar."

"Who's Amar?"

"Her lover. Haven't you heard?"

"No."

"Ask her about him sometime. She got involved with him back in Tunis."

"What, is he an Arab?"

"Worse," said the Gentleman. "Much worse. His father was an Arab, his mother was a Pole. Got mixed up in some rather shady business in Tunis. Naturally, he wound up in prison. 'He had some unpleasantness,' as Mishka would have said. It was she who bailed him out."

"Who?"

"Lida, of course. Are you surprised?"

"No, it all seems perfectly plausible."

"Only this is all strictly between you and me."

"You may rest assured."

There was, of course, nothing surprising about anything the Gentleman had told me; on the contrary, it would have been astonishing if there had been. Although I couldn't help feeling sorry for Pavel Alexandrovich. How was it that he knew so little about Lida? How could it be that, despite having such a clear recollection of the mousey marksman and Zina, he had left out the most important part—Lida's story? I learnt from the Gentleman that Pavel Alexandrovich had until quite recently only known of Lida from hearsay, but when he met her for the first time in the street he was moved by her unmistakeable poverty and misery—this was where everything had started. She would doubtless have told him about herself, but only what she deemed necessary to tell, concealing the rest from him. Moreover, he was thirty years her senior, and yet his persistent mistrust of people and his own experience in life were powerless in the face of this age gap. Still, was he really capable of deceiving himself so much on her account? Never had I imagined that Zina's daughter would turn out to be a wistful girl with distant eyes, but the moment I laid eyes on her and heard her singing, I had no doubt as to her moral character. That Pavel Alexandrovich did not recognize—or at least made out not to recognize—something so obvious could only be put down to his catastrophic, involuntary blindness.

Several weeks passed. Then one evening, completely by chance, I found myself on Place de la Bastille, just as I had done when I came across Zina, the mousey marksman and Lida on Boulevard Garibaldi. It had been a long time since I was last in this quarter of Paris. I was there because a famous Spanish revolutionary was due to give a speech at one of the larger cafés in the area; his views had long been a subject of interest to me because they lacked the naive stupidity one invariably encounters in political orators. His lecture was to be on socialism and the proletariat; he was a brilliant man, and in his analysis these things took on a human dimension. Listening to him, I was struck by the degree to which the true essence of these questions had been corrupted and distorted by ignorant, stupid politicians, who for whatever reason considered themselves representatives of the working class, while presiding over syndicates, parties and governments. The lecture finished just after eleven o'clock in the evening. As I crossed the square, passing the notorious Rue de Lappe with its ubiquitously advertised dens, a red taxi pulled up at the corner; out of it stepped Lida, followed by a man of average height, wearing a grey suit, with a dark, thin face and a grey hat pulled down almost to his ears. From a distance he reminded me of the owner of Mishka's hotel, although not because they bore any physical similarity to one another, but because—in as far as I was able to discern in those few seconds—there was something currish and criminal about his face. What served to underscore such an impression was his look of severe stupidity; it was obvious that this man was unaccustomed to and even incapable of thinking. Next to him, Lida's delicate face seemed almost abstract. My eyes met her gaze, but I pretended not to see or recognize her; she too made as if she hadn't recognized me. I quickly walked past them, but then stopped to watch where they were headed—towards the illuminated entrance of a dance hall. To my surprise I noticed that Amar—I had no doubt that this was he—walked very slowly, slightly dragging his left leg.

This happened on a Wednesday. The following Saturday evening I was due to dine at Pavel Alexandrovich's. On Thursday, when he and I arranged everything over the telephone and he asked me how I was getting on, I replied that I had hardly been out, as I had been so busy with work. Indeed this was the case: I had recently been writing a lengthy piece on the Thirty Years War, which a friend of mine had been commissioned to write, but which he in turn had passed on to me. The article was to be published under the name of a very famous columnist and writer, a man of means, who had earned a considerable fortune from writing books about the dictators and government ministers of various countries. I was not entirely convinced that he himself could have written such an article; however, I was personally unacquainted with him and can only defer to my friend's categorical assertion that the famous author "was unburdened with knowledge in any quarter, save for the noble sport of horse racing". However, this was not the crux of the matter; rather it lay in the fact that the famous journalist was having a tempestuous affair with a no less famous actress of the silver screen. He would go with her to all the fashionable late-night cabarets, whisk her off to Italy and the Riviera—in brief, he had no time at all for any articles. Besides, this was not the first time in his life that such a thing had happened. One way or another, the chance for me to earn some money was much too tempting to pass up. I spent several days in the Bibliothèque Nationale, copying out long passages from a variety of books, then I set to work at home. I still had a long way to go before I would reach the closing pages, however, and I was pondering the Peace of Westphalia with no less trepidation than did Richelieu, albeit with one marked difference: I knew its consequences, which the French cardinal along with his contemporaries could not have foreseen and in light of which the whole of early seventeenth-century French politics had acquired a rather different significance than was ascribed to it by either the cardinal or even Père Joseph, who had been at least on the face of it so terribly unselfish. But the more I thought about the old barefooted Capuchin, the more unquestionable it seemed that only boundless, hidden ambition could have ordained both his politics and his life. The argument of one historian of this period seemed awfully convincing to me; he wrote that the most dangerous people in politics are those who scorn the direct advantages resulting from their positions, who strive towards neither personal wealth nor the satisfaction of traditional passions, whose sense of individuality finds its expression in the defence of some idea or historical concept. Unfortunately I was deprived of the opportunity to express my personal views on the Thirty Years War, and the need to adopt a certain writing style impeded me and hindered my work. The fate of Gustavus Adolphus in particular had to be abandoned without any detailed commentary, as did the part played by Wallenstein, whose grandiose, chaotic plans, however, were in my opinion more deserving of attention than Richelieu's policies. I was further hindered by the fact that in contrast to the journalist whose name was to appear alongside the article and who was completely indifferent to the fate of any historical figure, just as he was to any historical concept, I was intrigued by the fates of all the political actors and military leaders who had taken part in the war. Despite the three hundred years separating me from them, I came to feel for each of them what any of their contemporaries might have done—although I was acutely aware that in the various historians' accounts these figures were no less distorted and stylized than had they been transformed by Schiller's muse. It seemed impossible to treat Richelieu with anything but scorn, in the same way that it was impossible to write of Père Joseph with anything but respect. I tried to search for some hidden meaning in the fate of Tilly, the suicide of Wallenstein and particularly in the death of Gustavus Adolphus—but of course these notions were entirely misplaced in such a work. When I later had occasion to meet with the dummy author of the article—he turned out to be fat, bald and middle-aged, forever short of breath and with dull eyes— he was truly astonished by what I had come up with. I think that his disagreement with me over my appraisal of certain historical aspects would have been more pointed if he had held the slightest relevant idea about the content of his article. He made a few alterations, but as time was of the essence he was forced to limit himself to the purely superficial: he inserted colons and exclamation marks everywhere he could, imparting a pretentious and didactic aspect to my account and introducing an element of bad taste which, I fancied, had not been there to begin with, but was unerringly characteristic of this ignorant and vulgar man.

But all this happened later; on Friday, however, at around three o'clock in the afternoon, while I was writing at my desk, there was a knock at the door. This surprised me, as I was not expecting anyone.

"Come in!" I said.

The door opened and there I saw Lida. She was dressed in a grey suit with a white, very low-cut blouse and a grey hat. Her eyes immediately fixed themselves on me, so that I felt fleetingly uncomfortable. I offered her the armchair. Then I asked her to what I owed the pleasure of this visit.

"I've come to you because I consider you to be a decent man."

"I'm flattered," I said somewhat impatiently. "Nevertheless, your visit no doubt has some more immediate purpose. Surely you haven't come just to give me your personal appraisal of my moral qualities?"

She continued looking straight at me; this unnerved me.

"We saw each other recently," she said.

"You are referring to the evening when we dined at Pavel Alexandrovich's?"

Her eyes contained a mixture of reproach and ennui, and then, for the very first time, it occurred to me that she might in fact not be as stupid as she looked.

"Are you quite sure that you want to speak to me in such a condescending tone, so blatantly giving me to know that you think I'm an idiot?"

She had switched into French; in Russian such a phrase would have been too difficult for her.

"Heaven forbid!"

"You spotted me on Place de la Bastille as I was arriving with my lover."

"Forgive me, but your personal life is no concern of mine."

"Yes, indeed," she said impatiently.

After her words about my having seen her in Place de la Bastille, her motives for coming here seemed clear enough.

"I'm afraid you're wasting your time," I said. "You're hoping that I won't mention it to anyone, am I correct?"

She grimaced, as though swallowing something unpalatable.

"Yes."

"Now see here," I said. "Allow me to be perfectly frank with you. You don't want Pavel Alexandrovich to know about this because you're afraid of losing your position. I too don't want him to learn of this, but for a somewhat different reason: I pity him."

"But don't you understand?"

"Let's not, shall we? Pursuing this would not be to your advantage."

She then launched into an unexpected and malicious tirade.

"No, of course you don't understand. *Parce que, voyez-vous, vous êtes un monsieur.** No one's ever slapped you in the face. No one's ever called you a whore."

* Because, you see, you're a man.

101

"*On se tromperait de sexe.*"*

"Shut up and let me speak. You've never had to walk the streets; you've never had to live for weeks without knowing where you'll be spending the night. You've never been manhandled by the police. You've never had to spend nights with flea-ridden Arabs. You don't know the meaning of a native quarter; you haven't breathed in its air. You don't understand what it means to have to depend on some fat, drooling client."

Her speech was disjointed, her voice low and hoarse.

"You don't know what it is to hate your own mother. You don't know what it is to live your life in poverty. You just go to university, attending lectures, sleeping in a clean bed and sending your washing out to the laundry. *On m'a traînée toute la vie dans la boue, moi.*"†

She paused. Her face betrayed an expression of weariness.

"Before, when I was alone, I used to cry. I'd cry from despair, from poverty, from the fact that there was nothing I could do about it. When I was a girl, I cried because my mother's lover would beat her, and she would cry with me. What do you know about me? Nothing. Yet when you speak to me, your voice is full of contempt; do you think I can't hear it? Yes, I understand: we belong to two different worlds—*nous appartenons à deux mondes différents.*"

---

* Perhaps because I'm the wrong sex.

† My whole life I've been dragged through the mud.

"You must have read that somewhere," I said calmly.

"Perhaps. But all the same, you don't know the first thing about me."

And so she began talking of her life. By her account, she truly had known nothing but poverty and degradation. Her mother used to send her out to collect fag ends in the street. Zina's lover would beat them both. They would sing in the streets and in courtyards, where people would chase them away—they would sing in autumn, in the rain, and in winter, as the chill winds blew. They often had nothing to eat but what they could find in Les Halles. Lida had taken her first bath at the age of fifteen.

Then, when everything became too unbearable, she left home and went to Marseilles. She had no money for the ticket, so she paid for everything "in other ways", as she phrased it. From Marseilles, she travelled on to Tunis.

There she spent four years. She spoke of the sultry African nights, of how she had gone for days on end without food and, without mincing her words, of what the Arabs had made her do. The more she spoke, the more I understood what until now I had only suspected—that she was ridden with vice and poverty and that she had spent her whole life in some stinking hell. She had been punched in the face, in the body and in the head, and she had even endured the cuts of a knife. She unbuttoned her blouse and below her breasts, held fast in their brassiere, I glimpsed white scar tissue. She had never been educated, although she did possess a good memory. In Tunis she had worked for a while as a maid to an old doctor, whose apartment contained a library; in the evenings she would read the books she borrowed from there, and the more she read—she claimed—the more dismal her own life seemed to her. Then she met Amar, who was ill and similarly down on his luck. He was suffering acutely from consumption and could no longer work. She stayed on with the doctor and spent every penny she earned on Amar, who, thanks to her nursing and care, began to convalesce. Even so, he was unable to return to his former work.

I had been listening to her without interrupting, but on this point I asked:

"Where was he working before? What had he been doing?"

"I don't know," she said. "In some factory, I think."

She said she loved this man more than anything else in the world and was ready to lay down her life for him.

"The need seldom arises in such cases," I said. "This is hardly the libretto of some opera. By the way, why does he limp?"

"How do you know that?"

"I've seen him walk."

Again she stared straight at me, and for the first time I noticed the menacing look in her eyes.

"He had an accident," she said.

Later the doctor let her go and so she returned to Paris, where she met Pavel Alexandrovich. It happened in the street, at dusk; she had been sitting on a bench, crying because Amar was still in Tunis and lacked the funds to make the journey to join her. Pavel Alexandrovich had asked her why she was crying. She explained to him that she felt wretched. Though she made no mention of Amar. He invited her into a café and spoke to her as no one had ever done before. Then he gave her some money and said that if she was ever in need, she could come to him or call him on the telephone. It was not difficult to guess the rest. Pavel Alexandrovich, according to Lida, would take her to the Louvre, teach her many things she did not know, and give her books that he thought interesting to read.

In spite of the clear effort she was making to speak kindly of Pavel Alexandrovich, her animosity towards him still seeped through. I imagine she despised him for his gullibility and loathed the idea that he was superior to Amar. She expressed herself rather differently, saying that she was grateful to Pavel Alexandrovich, but, naturally, she could never love him. She was incapable of loving him, and I ought to understand this—but at the same time she could not live without love.

"Now tell me, don't I deserve at least a little happiness—even at the price of deceit?"

Her penchant for using literary turns of phrase stolen from bad novels—especially during moments of pathos—irritated me somewhat. When she talked about Tunis, about her hatred for her mother, about the beatings, about her entire wretched life, she spoke in simple, precise terms.

"Now I'm at your mercy," she said. "You've heard all there is to know about me; my fate and that of the man I love depends on you. You know you may ask of me all that I can give, and you know I cannot refuse you."

Now I looked at her as I had never done before. I saw her legs in their stockings, the flexion of her body in the armchair, her heavy eyes, her delicate face, her red mouth and blonde hair tumbling down to her shoulders. I vividly recalled that evening at the cinema and what had come afterwards, her naked body reflected in a multitude of mirrors. The room felt both cold and stifling at the same time. I closed my eyes and thought of many things—and for a moment I felt truly sorry for her. She possessed only one means of payment for everything, and she was prepared to pay in order to protect what she called love, which was nothing but an irresistible attraction to that currish invalid, Amar. I remembered his face; it was peculiarly expressive in the sense that it had his destiny inscribed on it. A single glance was enough to know that this was the face of a doomed man and that the life awaiting him would not be a long one; either he would die of tuberculosis or he would perish on account of some other ailment, or perhaps he would be killed in some settling of scores and his body would be picked up by the police—with his throat slit or a bullet in his chest. Such, in any case, was my impression of him, and nothing could shake this. Lida's life, too, was tied to his fate. However, neither was in my hands; here she was mistaken.

Even if my mind had not been occupied by those recent visions of Wallenstein and Gustavus Adolphus—visions that had been interrupted by Lida's arrival—and reflections on Amar and the unrelenting notion of his being her lover—even had it not been for all this, her words, "You know I cannot refuse you," would still have had a sobering effect on me because they had sounded so unambiguous.

Then Lida began to dissolve, and in her place I saw a blurred white spot; a faint ringing started in my ears and it felt as if everything around me had become weightless and unreal. It was like the onset of a fainting fit, which somehow held the seduction of impending sweet oblivion. I made an effort to overcome it, lit a cigarette, inhaled several times and said:

"I won't detain you any longer. However, I do wish to say a few words to you. Firstly, I don't need anything from you; remember this once and for all. Secondly, we do indeed, as you said, belong to two different worlds, and in the world where I live people do not blackmail each other, they do not write anonymous letters, and they do not under any circumstances go about informing on one another. Perhaps if they had led a life like yours it would be a different story. That you have a right to happiness is your own affair; I consider it a very poor happiness. But if that is sufficient for you, one can only envy you. If I were asked to give up my world for the one in which you live, I'd sooner put a bullet through my brains."

I then stood up and added:

"I wish you all the best. You may rest assured that your visit and this conversation will remain strictly between the two of us."

After she left, something trembled and disappeared. For several seconds the room was quiet and deserted. Then I heard a mute, amorphous rumble, and it dawned on me that I was watching a battle whose outcome had been decided long ago, being impossible to alter or defer; it was the Battle of Lützen, which had played such a crucial part in the history of the Thirty Years War.

At this juncture of my life, time was passing by almost unnoticed; it was one of the least stable concepts I knew. Only later did I realize that my strength was being consumed by the constant pressure I found myself under, which was a reflection of some deep unrelenting internal struggle. It existed predominantly in the depths of my consciousness, in its dark recesses, beyond the control of logic. I sometimes began to feel as if I were close to victory, approaching the day when all these painful visions would vanish without trace. In any case, they were becoming ever more indistinct now; vague fragments of someone's life would flash before my eyes without having time to crystallize, and each time my return to reality would come quicker than it did before. Yet victory still eluded me: at times everything would suddenly grow dim and blurred; the noise of the street and the chatter of people would disappear—and then, with mute terror, I would await the return of one of those prolonged nightmares I had so recently known. This would go on for several minutes before the hum of the street rushed back to my ears and I was overcome by a brief tremor—then finally there would be calm.

Weeks and months passed in a similar manner. In the summer Pavel Alexandrovich and Lida escaped to Fontainebleau, where he persisted in inviting me although I never went. I stayed on in Paris, entirely alone, spending the majority of my time reading and going on long walks; I had no money to go anywhere. Then autumn came, and a wintery chill blew in from a window that had been left ajar. I spent the whole month of January in a state of unaccountable, distressing languor; each morning I would awake with a foreboding of catastrophe, and each day would pass without mishap. This feeling unnerved and wearied me, and only occasionally did I manage to rid myself of it and become the person I wanted to be: a normal man, unthreatened by either psychological attacks or fits of madness. Which was essentially what I felt whenever I found myself at Pavel Alexandrovich's.

One cold February evening I was having dinner at his apartment. Lida was absent. He and I were sitting at the table together, and he was in a contemplative mood. We then moved into his study; coffee had been served and there was a bottle of very strong, sweet wine, of which I took a few sips, although he, as usual, didn't touch a drop. He had donned a velvet smoking jacket, but was still wearing a shirt with a starched collar. As I looked at him I mused on how the happiest period of his life was probably the very one he was experiencing right now, how he had never known better times. It seemed impossible to think that this impression could be in any way erroneous. Everything about him—his movements, at once slow and certain, his gait, his bearing, the intonations in his voice, which seemed deeper and more expressive than before—confirmed such an assessment. It was very warm in his study, especially since the fire had been lit in addition to the central heating; the heavy curtains by the window billowed ever so slightly in the gentle breeze. I sat in an armchair, gazing into the fire. Then I shifted my eyes onto Pavel Alexandrovich and said:

"You know, as I look at this little fire, time seems to be regressing imperceptibly, farther and farther, and the more it regresses, the more I undergo subtle changes—and so now I find myself sitting naked and covered in hair at the entrance to some smoky Stone Age cave, by a fire laid by one of my far-distant ancestors. It's a charming picture of atavism."

"It is my belief that we do not exist beyond atavism," he said. "Everything that belongs to us, everything we know, everything we feel, we receive temporarily from the dead."

"Temporarily?"

"Of course. How could it be any otherwise?"

The hot flame flickered beneath the coals, and I could hear the gentle crackling of their combustion. I was feeling drowsy from the heat. Pavel Alexandrovich said:

"I've been thinking more and more about death recently. Not because I foresee it in the near future, but probably because I'm at a venerable age and it's natural, my young friend, to think about death at my stage in life. The most astonishing thing is that I think about it without the least fright or distress."

"Presumably because these thoughts are of a purely abstract nature."

"Not only that, I think. There's a certain seductiveness about the prospect, something majestic and of the utmost significance. Remember the words of the requiem: 'rest in the bosom of Abraham, Isaac and Jacob…'"

"In the bosom of Abraham, Isaac and Jacob…" I immediately saw before me the echoing vaults of a church rising up, a coffin with the body of an unknown man, the priest, the deacon, the censers, the icons, the motion-less flight of gilded angels on the Royal Gates of the iconostasis, and the inscription high up above the angels, above this thousand-year history of Christianity: "Come unto me, all ye that labour and are heavy laden, and I will give you rest."

"Do you believe in God, Pavel Alexandrovich?"

"I didn't so much before, but now I do. He who has known years of poverty will find it easier to believe than any other man. Because, you see, Christianity is the religion of the poor, and that is why the Gospels contain words to this effect, as I'm sure you'll recall."

"Yes," I said. "But I also remember a great deal more. I once had occasion to read a most edifying encyclical by a pope—I forget which—who argued that one must know how to interpret the Church's views on wealth and poverty correctly. Specifically, there could be no talk of donating one's wealth, or even a tenth of it, to the poor: this was a misinterpretation. The tenth pertained to income; capital was never subject to Christian taxation. This is patently ridiculous, and if there is a hell, then I hope this pope, while he's sat there, roasting for centuries in some gigantic frying pan, has found the time to realize his grievous error concerning the Church's stance on property."

"I used to believe I would die just like my friends in Rue Simon le Franc," continued Shcherbakov. "That is to say, my body would have been found at dawn one winter's morning, somewhere near the Seine, by a bench, covered in frost. That was only to be expected."

A small shaded lamp lit up his face, serene and contemplative.

"And you know, I always used to find the thought objectionable; enviously I'd look on at lavish funerals, until one day I thought: I'd like to die like that. So that's how I often imagine my own end now, not without a certain—how shall I say?—comfort: a will, a notary, a long illness that teaches me humility and prepares me for the final journey, the last sacraments, the obituary in the newspaper: 'We regret to announce the death of Pavel Alexandrovich Shcherbakov…', then the date and time of the funeral."

"Now wait just one moment, Pavel Alexandrovich," I said. "What sort of macabre creation is this? And anyway, as far as I recall, you have no close friends or acquaintances, not counting your more recent associates of course. You have no one to leave a will for. And who'll come to your funeral? From a purely practical perspective, as it were, and forgive me for being so blunt, but these dreams of yours seem rather fanciful to me."

"Perhaps," he answered distractedly. "But I assure you, they aren't devoid of a certain pleasure."

I admitted that, although I could understand this from a theoretical stance, I found it difficult to accept. I said that I always imagined death to be a catastrophe—momentary or slow, sudden or natural, but a catastrophe nonetheless—a spectre of otherworldly terror that made one's blood run cold. The notion of there being some comfort in this was entirely alien to me. He remarked that such a view at my age—he emphasized this point—was understandable, and asked incidentally whether I had a conscious dislike of cemeteries.

"No," I said. "I suppose there's something calming about them."

As we spoke of this, I remembered being in an army camp on the banks of the Dardanelles long ago; one day I was assigned to a grave-digging detachment. I told this to Pavel Alexandrovich. The man in charge of the cemetery was an old colonel with moustaches, who spoke with a strong Caucasian accent. He would come up to me, inspect my work and say:

"Dig! Dig, my boy! Dig deeper. Dig *as deep as you can.*"

When he came over one last time, he found me standing at the bottom of a rectangular pit one and a half times the height of a grown man. It was already approaching evening.

"That's enough now," he said. "Climb out of there, my boy."

"Colonel, sir," I said. "May I ask—who exactly am I doing this last service for? Who's to be buried in this grave?"

He made a vague gesture with his hand.

"I don't know yet, my boy. I just don't know. We're all in God's hands. If you should die tomorrow, my boy, why, it's you we'll bury."

Many years later I learnt that this colonel had ended up as a labourer in France, dying somewhere near Roubaix.

In that moment I pitied that it hadn't happened on the banks of the Dardanelles and that he hadn't been lowered into the pit I had dug in the warm clay soil that yielded so readily under the gravedigger's shovel; it would have spared him the long years of an unhappy life, and perhaps, had he died then, he might have managed to hold on to some of the illusions whose fallacy had been revealed to him only because he died too late.

"Perhaps," said Pavel Alexandrovich. "But perhaps not."

The conversation now turned to other matters. Pavel Alexandrovich recounted memories of his youth, and I particularly remember—perhaps because I envisaged it with a peculiar clarity—one of his adventures, albeit of little importance. One winter's day, in the north of Russia, he had been walking through a forest—this was not long before the Revolution, when he was still an officer. Suddenly his bulldog, which had been running ahead of him, began barking ferociously. He looked up and spotted a lynx sitting stock-still in a nearby tree. At the time, Pavel Alexandrovich was wearing an officer's greatcoat and carrying a sabre and a revolver. He shot at the lynx, but instead of killing it only wounded it—then, in one gigantic leap, the lynx pounced at him. He took a step back in the nick of time and the lynx landed on all fours right in front of him, whereupon the bulldog immediately tore into it. Pavel Alexandrovich elected not to shoot, afraid of wounding the dog, so he took his sabre and slashed open the lynx's stomach as the dog clamped its jaws around its throat. The snow turned red with blood, and against the pink sunset of a winter's day crows were circling slowly above. Before me I saw the lynx's dead grin, the virgin whiteness of the snow that had been disturbed in the struggle, and the young officer with a sabre in his hand. Now I looked at his face—it wore a weary, peaceful expression—and I thought how many years had passed since that Russian winter, and in so doing I perceived the seemingly unstoppable onward march of time.

Then began talk of travel, and Pavel Alexandrovich said that he was intending—if everything went according to plan—to emigrate to Canada, far away from Europe, her political paroxysms and the constant feeling of vague anxiety that filled the air we breathed.

"Just think," he said. "Here, every stone is dripped in blood. Wars, revolutions, barricades, crimes, despotic regimes, inquisitions, famine, devastation and this whole historical gallery of horrors—the fate of Bohemia, St Bartholomew's Night, Napoleon's soldiers in Spain— do you recall the series of drawings by Goya? Europe is like a murderer, haunted by bloody visions and remorse, just waiting for even more state-led crimes. No, I'm too old for all that; I'm tired. I long for warmth and peace. For so many years I went cold and hungry, without hope, in the vague anticipation of death or some miracle, so now I believe I've earned the right to some repose and certain illusory, sentimental consolations—the last I'm ever likely to know."

Illusory consolations. Yes, there was no better way of putting it. So he did understand, despite his recent blindness; even that villainous shadow across Lida's face, which, every time I saw her, aroused within me both fear and revulsion at the same time as it did an incomprehensible and humiliating attraction to her—even that had not escaped his eyes.

"And you? How have you been lately?" he asked.

I told him that I was still fumbling my way, as it were, through a causeless, unremitting state of almost metaphysical malaise, and that I felt at times such spiritual fatigue as if I had lived for ever.

"Something is the matter with you, dear friend," he said. "To look at, however, one would think you're perfectly fine. Perhaps you should take some rest by the sea or in the countryside. Have a think about it."

I shrugged and glanced over at the bookshelves. For the first time I noticed a little yellow statue that I was unable to make out properly. I asked Pavel Alexandrovich what it was. He got up from his armchair, picked it up and handed it to me.

It was a solid gold statuette of the Buddha, with a rather large oval ruby at its navel. I was struck most by the figure's pose: contrary to what I was used to seeing, it was depicted not sitting, but standing upright. Both its arms were raised aloft, without any bend at the elbows whatsoever; its bald head was tilted slightly to one side, the eyelids drooped heavily over the eyes, its mouth lay open, and the face wore an expression of austere ecstasy, which was conveyed with extraordinary power. At its golden stomach, with a mysterious, deathly significance, the ruby glittered dimly. The statuette was so remarkable that I just kept staring at it, unable to tear myself away, entirely forgetting where I was. Finally I said:

"A splendid piece. Where did you come by it?"

He said that he had bought it recently in Paris, in one of the antique shops.

"I often find myself looking at it," he said, "and of course every time it makes me think of Buddhism, which rather appeals to me."

"A tempting religion, I find."

"Exceedingly so. You and I are Christians by an accident of history; we Russians could have made excellent Buddhists."

What he then said to me seemed questionable—perhaps because in such arguments it is difficult to avoid several arbitrary generalizations. Moreover, I was inclined to think that almost all religions, with the exception of a handful of barbaric cults, agreed on certain points, and the ecstasy of the Buddha, for example, which had been communicated with such persuasiveness in this golden statuette, reminded me of several paintings in the Louvre—in particular, the exultant face of St Jerome.

"Yes, this is what one must strive towards," said Shcherbakov. "One must reach an understanding of nirvana. Before, I used to think that it was like looking into a dark bottomless pit, but then I realized my error."

Perhaps, I thought, I ought to become a Buddhist—principally because of this striving towards nirvana. I told Pavel Alexandrovich that in moments of extreme psychological anguish, I would invariably experience a desire to dissolve and disappear.

"I think," I said, half in jest, half in all earnestness, "that if I were able to tell the Buddha about this, the great sage would take pity on me."

In spite of the late hour, we sat discussing a great variety of subjects: Buddhism, Dürer's paintings, Russia, literature, music, hunting, the crunch of snow that has turned to ice, the streak of moonlight that ripples on the ocean's surface, the poor who were dying in the streets, the daily life of cripples, America's urban civilization, the foul stench of Versailles, the ignorant, villainous tyrants who so often ruled the world, and the inevitable and loathsome apocalyptic devastation apparently inherent in every era of human history.

* * *

It was precisely ten minutes to one when I left. I remember this because I glanced at my watch and momentarily thought, in the false light of the street lamp, that it was five minutes past ten, which surprised me. But then I took a closer look and realized my mistake. Perhaps I could have caught the last service on the Métro, but I decided to walk nonetheless. It was a cold, starry night; here and there along the pavements glimmered streaks of frozen water. I surveyed my surroundings distractedly as I continued along the familiar road, then I looked straight ahead of me and saw amid the yellowish winter mist that the streets and their lamps had mysteriously disappeared. I paused, lit a cigarette and looked about myself. Truly, there were no buildings or streets at all: I found myself standing in the middle of a bridge across the Seine. Leaning against the railing, I stood there for a long time, gazing at the dark surface of the river. It flowed silently between those statues of the water nymphs that I had failed to recognize on my return from the nonexistent prison in that imaginary state. As I looked down at the water I gradually forgot all about my contemplative faculties' unfortunate limitations, which I was always conscious of unless there was sky or water in front of me. Whenever I beheld either of these, I would begin to feel as if I were no longer pent in on all sides—by time, circumstance, the imperfection of my senses, the personal and insignificant details of my life, my own physical traits. Only then would I feel as if my mind were unburdened, as if freedom's reflection were approaching me, fulfilling some divine promise—amid this silent, magisterial infinity of water or air. Whatever I thought of in these moments, my mind functioned differently than it did normally and acquired a certain detachment from the external circumstances affecting it. Sometimes I would forget where these thoughts had begun; at other times they would remain fixed in my mind. I knew, however, that I would never discover their mysterious, long-lost origin, which had vanished in the mute stillness of time gone by. I would feel as if I were now a spectator, somewhere amid this expanse of air or water, to the perpetual motion of that indefinable mass of the most diverse things—objects and thoughts, stone buildings and memories, street corners and expectations, optical impressions and despair—through which passed both my own life and those of other people, my brothers and contemporaries.

And so I thought of the strange allure contained in this longing for my own disappearance. What seemed seductive to me might have been so for others, too, and particularly for Pavel Alexandrovich. Perhaps it was not by chance that he had spoken about Buddhism, which, as he saw it, led to an almost complete liberation from our impermanent, earthly shell. It was necessary to overcome this persistent oppressive state: the essential dependence of our spiritual life on some sordid physical substance that filters our perception of the world and is ultimately unworthy of fulfilling this "solemn mission", as he had termed it. A man who thinks like this must surely have experienced some imbalance in his mental equilibrium, he will have heard the far-distant call of another world, abstract and sublime like the end of time, of which the holy books speak so insistently. Compared to this, of what value was this meagre aggregate of sensual pleasures that were left to him? Had he been a few decades younger, had he been possessed of a strong heart, enormous lungs and the muscular strength of a young athletic body, then perhaps this pagan frenzy of earthly passions would have rendered him impervious to Buddhism and meditation alike.

As happened so often—perhaps precisely because I was twenty-five and knew nothing of physical handicap, and for me the sensual world was no less attractive than the spiritual one—my thoughts were cut short by a visual memory. Before my eyes appeared the two glass circles of my field binoculars, through which I found myself observing a cavalry attack bearing down upon us—that is, my comrades and me—during the war in Russia. I could see the cavalrymen approaching us in close forma-tion, the rapid, rhythmic undulation of this live mass of horses and riders; watching it with baited breath, unable to tear myself away, it revealed the seemingly irresistible power of youth and muscle. This was an attack of the victors: it was a victory over death and over the fear of death, because it was madness and because machine guns and cannon were aimed at these men armed only with rifles and sabres. No thought, no argument could put a halt to this blind will to self-oblivion. With a feeling of profound pity I took the binoculars away from my eyes, for the riders were already two hundred metres away and at any moment artillery and dozens of machine guns would open fire on them. Moments later waves of them would be mown down, and on the scorched grass of the rolling field would lie only corpses and the dying. Nothing remained of all this but the two glass circles of my field binoculars, preserved in time and space and reflected now in the retreating surface of a night-time river in a distant foreign city, as well as that recurring weight in my heart and the memory of these fallen victors who, after so many years, had commenced their senseless, heroic attack once more in my mind.

The dark waters continued to flow silently before my eyes. Again my thoughts turned to Pavel Alexandrovich. What would remain in life if one were to remove the base pleasures resulting from purely physical sensations—warmth, food, bed, Lida, sleep? The exultant face of the Buddha? The ecstasy of St Jerome? The death of Michelangelo? What could this biological tremor of existence signify to a man who has known the cold allure of oblivion? "And I saw a new heaven and a new earth: for the first heaven and the first earth were passed away; and there was no more sea." If one were to look upon it as a spectator, what was happening here and now was particularly absurd: winter, February, Paris, a bridge over the Seine, eyes cast down at the dark river, and a mute stream of thoughts, images and words in an incredible mix of time and thought. Pavel Alexandrovich, Lida and her entire life, the Buddha, St Jerome and the Revelation of St John, the cavalry attack, the binoculars, oblivion, and the random physical appearance of a man in a navy-blue overcoat resting his elbows on the heavy railings, the fragile physical shell that encases a part of this mysterious range of movements.

Just then something twitched inside me—I cannot describe it any other way. My gaze, which had until now been fixed on a single point in the river, slid farther away, and the shimmering reflections of the street lamps floated into my field of vision. I looked up from the river, and then with phenomenal speed the stars in the winter sky appeared before me, cold and distant. Perhaps I am still destined to awaken one day or one evening, to forget these abstract terrors and to begin living as I once did and as I ought to live always, not in the fantasy that surrounded me, but in the immediate reality of existence. Oblivion never entirely forsook me; it merely receded a little into the distance. This almost allowed me to forget all about it, and thus I would begin to perceive everything differently: when spending the night with a woman I would feel a sense of gratitude towards my poor body, when reading some third-rate novel I would no longer despise the dead man who had written it. In a certain sense, it began to seem as if everything—or almost everything—had a justification of its own and that, surrounded by this scant human warmth, I was living in a world where people cried when a baby died or a husband was killed on the battlefield, where people said, "I've never loved anyone but you," in a world full of children and puppies, in a world beyond which lay only coldness and death.

Suddenly I felt chilled to the bone; I upturned the collar of my overcoat and crossed the bridge. Yet I kept thinking about Pavel Alexandrovich and his ultimately astonishing fate. I recalled his saying to me that he had been saved by this obscure illness, and the more I thought about it, the more I was inclined to believe that his abstinence from wine, all the pain and retching, was perhaps not even an illness, but some mysterious manifestation of man's instinct for self-preservation, the very thing that his unfortunate comrades had been so lacking in. What would have become of his inheritance had he remained an alcoholic? Again I saw him standing in front of me, just as he had been when I first laid eyes on him—an old beggar in the Jardin du Luxembourg. Those words of his, which had been uncomfortable to hear and which he had uttered long after becoming rich, rang in my ears:

"I shan't return to you the ten francs you gave me back then; that would be no way to thank you. I was so very grateful to you for it. I know, of course, that you're more or less indifferent to money, but people seldom give so much to an old beggar."

Now he would be sitting in his armchair, in his warm, well-appointed apartment, looking at his bookshelves and the golden Buddha, thinking on a peaceful death. Lida would come in the evening and render up her obedient body to him; then she would arise from his bed and return to her flat, and he would sleep until the morning—in those white bedsheets, under the quilted duvet. In the morning he would drink some coffee and read the newspaper, later he would take lunch and then go out, either on foot or by car, for a walk. In the evening he would go sometimes to the theatre, sometimes to a concert, sometimes to the cinema. He had no concerns about tomorrow, money or the future in general; there was everlasting warmth and comfort, a fireplace, divans, armchairs, and soft footsteps across the thick-piled rug in his study. How absurd all of this might have seemed to him even two years ago, as he wandered about Paris during those cold winter days, occasionally ducking into the warm, foul-smelling Métro. If you had said to him then that he would presently be living as he did now... Then again, there had been nothing miraculous or incredible about it. It had come about simply because one day, one and a half or two thousand kilometres from Paris, the sea had been rather cold, and a cruel, miserly old man who was swimming not even very far from the shore had experienced a fateful cramp, leaving him to sink down to the seabed, his lungs filling with water, and die. There was nothing to it, apart from a most natural series of facts: the water temperature in the North Sea, a tendency towards arthritis in men of a certain age, an inadequate knack for swimming or, perhaps, a sudden stroke.

"Rest in the bosom of Abraham, Isaac and Jacob…"
"There's something quite comforting about it all…" Suddenly it struck me that these words contained an infinitely sad truth. Perhaps it would be better if he were to die right now, just as it would have been better for my commandant to have died back then in Greece, and not much later in a factory town in France. At long last he, Pavel Alexandrovich Shcherbakov, had found true happiness. But who knows what could happen next. He might grow used to such comfort and stop appreciating it; it might seem as if he had always lived like this and what happened to him was dull and commonplace. He would soon be in his sixties, and presently those cruel hardships he had endured would begin taking their toll; there would be ailments, illnesses, doctors, all the burdens that old age brings, and the irreversible awareness that money had come too late: instead of desire there would be pain, instead of appetite an aversion to food, instead

of deep sleep lingering insomnia. Yes, it would be better for him to die right now. He had known everything: youth, the dawning of strength, the spectre of death on the battlefield, passion, wine, poverty, man's steepest fall and his triumphant return to a world that had long been inaccessible to him, the incredible journey from having recollections to being recollected, from nothingness to life. What was left for him—within the confines of human existence? No rest could ever bring back his former strength, for time had robbed him of the chance to recover it: such miracles did not happen. Perhaps a truly worthy and timely conclusion to this existence would be the journey to the place where there is no "sorrow, nor any sighing, but life everlasting".

Perhaps that would have been best. Although personally I would have felt sorry for him. I liked his serenity, his genuine benevolence towards me, the intonations of his deep voice, his unaffected elegance—these were all qualities that he had borne through those cruel trials and succeeded in preserving just as they would be when youth and vigour permit a man the luxury of magnanimity. Would I have occasion to witness their gradual dissolution and to see before me not the current Pavel Alexandrovich, but an embittered old man, weary from chronic ailments and hateful of others because their own good health would let them comprehend neither his suffering nor his impotent rage?

I suddenly thought of the frenzied, ecstatic face of the Buddha with its arms raised aloft. Perhaps he saw before him a nirvana to which we were closer than we thought, which we took for granted, which we desired, towards which, in the depths of our consciousness, we even strove.

"Which we desired." Let us replace the plural with a singular: "Which I desired." Why, in some purely speculative domain, was I condemning Pavel Alexandrovich Shcherbakov to death, or to the approach of nirvana? Why was I in my imagination—as it could happen nowhere else, and my imagination was after all a distorted reflection of myself—deliberately and actively wishing for his death? Why was I conducting this theoretical assassination? And to what end was I responsible for this crime? For in the world to which my stubborn illness condemned me, the border between reality and abstraction, between deeds and ideas, was neither well defined nor fixed. I had, for instance, to make a phenomenal effort in order to remember whether Lida had in fact been mine—in that room of mirrors. How naive it would have been to think that my whole life, this long and complex journey whose origin was lost in a baffling mist, could perhaps be reduced to a sequence of overt external facts. The remainder, as vague and uncertain as it was, could be termed a departure from reality, delirium or madness. And yet it also contained a strange, undeniable coherence, passing from one fit of madness to the next—probably until the point where the last remnants of my consciousness would be swallowed up by the approaching darkness, and either I would vanish once and for all, or, after a long interval, like a coma lasting for many years, I would see myself again in some far-flung country, at the roadside, an unknown tramp with no name, no age, no nationality. Then perhaps I would be able to breathe freely and forget the criminal darkness of my imagination, the abstract odiousness of my depravity, and this theoretical assassination.

It had already gone two o'clock by the time I reached my hotel. Mado stopped me at the street corner and asked for a cigarette. Then she glanced at me and said:

"You've an odd look about you today. What's the matter, are you tired?"

"It's just the way the lamplight is falling on my face," I said. "No, I'm not tired. I just want to go to bed."

"Well, good night then."

"Good night, Mado."

I went up to my room and pulled the blanket off the divan; in the soft light the sheets and the pillowcases gleamed white. I remember that as I undressed I envisaged falling into a deep sleep and waking up in the morning, having forgotten all this unnecessary, imaginary nonsense.

*   *   *

I awoke, however, with a heavy head. After a cold shower and a shave I left my hotel. To the right of the entrance I was surprised to notice a dark-blue motor car of the type generally used by the police. Scarcely had I taken a few steps when I felt someone's hand at my shoulder. I turned around. Before me stood a broad man in a suit, with a flat, inexpressive face.

"You're under arrest," he said. "Follow me."

I was so stunned that for the first few seconds I was unable to say a single word. Presently a second man in a suit appeared; we got into the vehicle and set off. Only then did I ask:

"On what charges?"

"You ought to know that better than anyone else."

"I don't understand."

"Then let's hope there's been some misunderstanding that we can soon clear up."

The car stopped at the embankment of the Seine. I sat in a waiting room; one police inspector stayed with me, while the other left. He was gone for a long time. I sensed the weight in my head returning, and I felt a strange detachment from everything that was going on around me; I was struck by the similarity to the long hallucination that had led me to the building where I was remanded in custody in the imaginary Central State.

Eventually I was taken into another room, where an inspector was waiting for me. On both sides of his chair stood a number of men who all looked very similar to one another. The one who began questioning me had a clean-shaven, doleful face; he was no longer young, and wore a tired expression that he appeared to have assumed once and for all. He asked for my surname, my address, my occupation, my place and date of birth, and I gave him all the relevant answers. He looked me straight in the eye and suddenly asked, with a strange tone of reproach in his voice:

"Why did you kill him?"

That moment the ground seemed to slip away beneath my feet. Like a spectator to the event, I could see myself from a distance, walking along that street the previous night, and I remembered the pattern of my thoughts, which could have nothing to do with anything that was happening now. I shook my head and said:

"I'm sorry, I don't feel quite well and I haven't the faintest idea what you're talking about. Just what is it that you're trying to say?"

"I doubt this will come as any surprise to you. This morning Monsieur Shcherbakov was found dead in his apartment."

Again I felt delirious and devoid of the strength to overcome it. Naturally, I accepted the possibility that he had died; I was even inclined to think that it would have been to some degree timely at that very moment. Through a heavy mist two menacing human eyes stared threateningly and reproachfully at me; with a great effort I recalled that these belonged to the inspector.

"It was a purely theoretical supposition," I said. "It wasn't even a desire, it was just an arbitrary logical construct."

"Regrettably I fail to see anything theoretical about this. Shcherbakov has been murdered, stabbed in the back of the head. The blow was delivered from behind, while he was sitting in his armchair."

I stood up without raising my eyes. No, such a coincidence was out of the question. It was just an arbitrary logical construct, and I was ready to repeat it a thousand times over. No one but I could have known about it; my thoughts could not have been broadcast to some unknown assassin. And yet the times matched. No, of course this was impossible.

"But that's impossible," I said. And suddenly I realized that there could be no more dangerous a situation than the one I was in now. In the eyes of the inspector my words would take on an entirely different meaning, and if I kept up this dialogue with myself it would be the end of me.

"May I have a glass of water, please?" I asked.

He handed me a glass of water and a cigarette. Then he said:

"Of course, I'd be only too happy if it's proven that you aren't the murderer. But for that I need evidence, and so I must rely on you to help me."

"I'm sincerely grateful to you."

A policeman then arrived to conduct me to a photographer. I was placed on a revolving metal stool coated in white oil paint; the flashlight punched me in the face, and the stool swung in various directions as the camera clicked away. My fingers were then smeared with some black substance and pressed onto a sheet of white paper, after which I was escorted back.

Although it was fairly bright in the room where I was being questioned, they shone a lamp in my face that was almost as bright as those they had just used to photograph me. I recalled that this was a common method of interrogation.

The original inspector, however, was absent. In his place sat a man who was unknown to me, strikingly like the first, with a dark, sullen expression on his face.

"Well?" he said.

"I'm listening."

He grimaced from boredom and disgust.

"Let's get this over with," he said. "I need to go for lunch and you need a break. If you make a full and frank confession I'll try to help you. What were the motives for your crime?"

"I'd like to get out of this labyrinth," I said in response to my own thoughts.

"As would I. But that doesn't answer my question. I'll repeat it: what were the motives for your crime?"

I made a supreme effort to cross this border separating my thoughts on Pavel Alexandrovich's fate—thoughts that were evoked by a definite feeling of sympathy for him—from the facts that lay, or could lay, the blame squarely on me. I perfectly understood the profound difference between this dark sense of theoretical culpability and the thrust of a knife that had caused his death. I understood this, yet the combination of both one and the other was so powerful that in attempting to stick to the facts I felt as if I were forever stumbling into invisible walls barring me from even the simplest logical line of argument. I was unable to break free of this mental fog, although I knew that my next journey into it, as well as this absurd consciousness of my guilt—I realized the ridiculousness of it, but could do nothing to escape the sensation depriving me of the necessary presence of mind—threatened me with the most immediate and terrible danger.

The inspector posed several more questions that I was unable to answer with the necessary precision. He then left, only to be replaced by another. My eyes hurt from the glare of the lamp; I was thirsty, hungry and in need of a cigarette. Shortly after, I felt sleep begin to take hold of me; I nodded off for a brief moment and awoke to find someone tapping me on the shoulder. Another man I did not recognize asked me again what had driven me to murder. I took courage and replied once more that it was not a crime, but a logical construct. A familiar voice said:

"He's delirious from exhaustion, but he's still holding out."

Thereupon, however, the interrogation unexpectedly came to an end, and I was taken away. I walked like a drunk between the two policemen, swaying and stumbling. Then a door opened and I found myself in a narrow cell, on the floor of which lay a mattress covered by a blanket. I literally fell onto this, but sleep seemed to overcome me before I even touched it.

I awoke probably several hours later in total darkness, immediately recalling everything that had happened. I knew I was in prison and that I stood accused of Shcherbakov's murder. Only now did I truly comprehend it. Poor Pavel Alexandrovich, how short his enjoyment of the good life had been. But who could have murdered him, and more importantly why?

I spent almost three days trying vainly to regain my clarity of mind, which seemed forever to be slipping away, but the light, opaque mist that usually engulfed me during these strange episodes of mental illness refused to disperse. When I was finally called in for further questioning, I felt little better than I had done on the day of my arrest.

This time I found myself before an investigator, an elderly man with gentle eyes. After the initial formalities, he said:

"I have examined your file carefully, and there is nothing in it that affects you adversely. Do you deny murdering Shcherbakov?"

"Most categorically."

"You were on friendly terms with him, is that not correct?"

"Yes."

"Had you known him for long?"

"About three years."

"Do you remember where and when you first met him?"

I told him how I had come to know Pavel Alexandrovich.

"So he was a beggar in those days?"

"That's right."

"And three years later we find him living in a comfortable apartment on Rue Molitor? That sounds rather suspicious. How did it come about?"

I explained everything to him. I noticed that I found it much easier to answer his questions, and that the facts were more or less clear to me when the discussion had nothing to do with the murder.

"Very well," he said. "What were your movements on the evening of the eleventh of February, that is, the evening of Shcherbakov's murder? Can you remember your whereabouts?"

"Of course," I said. And indeed I vividly recalled everything that had happened: the cold evening, the occasional snowflake in the light of the street lamps, Odéon station, where I had begun my journey to Pavel Alexandrovich's, and my arrival at his apartment. I remembered the face of the conductor on the train, as well as that of the mechanic, and I would have recognized the passengers who were travelling in the same carriage as I was. I described everything to the investigator, right down to the menu for the dinner that Pavel Alexandrovich had served.

"Have you ever been engaged in any hard physical labour? Which trades do you know?"

I looked at him in astonishment, replying that, no, I had never done any hard physical labour and that I knew no trades. However, he seemed to attach no significance to this question, for he immediately said:

"After dinner you spent the whole evening chatting, is that not so?"

"Yes."

"Do you recall what you were talking about? This is very important."

At this point in the interrogation I was horrified suddenly to detect a gap in my memory. I was unable to remember anything of our conversation—it was as if it had never happened. Perspiration appeared on my forehead from the effort I was making to recall even some of what had been said that evening, and my head began to ache. I pulled myself together and said:

"Forgive me, but I'm in no fit state to remember anything right now. If you give me a little time, I'm sure it'll come back to me."

His eyes met my uneasy gaze. He was silent for a moment, then he nodded and finally said:

"Very well, try to tell me next time."

Once again I slept like a log for hours on end. When I awoke, I took a few steps about in the darkness. I hadn't felt like this in a long time. I was in a happy, almost forgotten state of physical and mental equilibrium, and it had come on so unexpectedly that I could scarcely believe my own senses. Catherine's distant face flashed before my eyes. I had nearly given up hope of seeing her again. What had happened to me during those hours, whose life veiled by heavy, impenetrable sleep had flitted past me, what had emerged out of this nothingness? How was it that what I had striven for at all costs, what I had so vainly expended this tremendous willpower on over the course of these interrogations, had suddenly revealed itself with such miraculous clarity in these few hours of sleep? Not only was I now unafraid of any interrogation, rather I looked forward to it.

When I was next brought before the investigator, the expression on his face was markedly graver than it had been on the previous occasion. I couldn't help but notice this, although it had none of the effect on me that it would undoubtedly have done even the night before.

"I must inform you," he began, "that your position has sharply deteriorated since we last spoke, which is to say nothing of the fact that we found no one else's fingerprints in Shcherbakov's apartment, except for yours and the deceased's."

He examined a piece of paper.

"There is a further aspect that doesn't bode well for you. Did you and Shcherbakov ever discuss his will?"

"Never," I said. "I'd be amazed to learn that he had ever given any thought to it."

"Nonetheless, his notary has provided us with a copy of the will: Shcherbakov has left his entire fortune to you."

"To me?" I said in astonishment. A chill ran down my spine. "That is indeed a terrible coincidence."

"The body of evidence stacked against you is almost too incredible to be believed," he said. "On the evening of the murder you went to Shcherbakov's. You are the last man to have seen him alive. No fingerprints other than yours have been found. Let us suppose that it's all a coincidence—an extremely unlucky one, but a coincidence nevertheless. The only argument to speak in your favour was that, as far as you were concerned, the murder would have been utterly pointless. Yet now we learn that there was a will, and this will leaves the deceased's entire fortune to you. The logical missing link—how you stand to benefit from Shcherbakov's death—has been found. You must admit that the evidence is overwhelming. And the answer to the question that arose at the very beginning—'Why did you kill him?'—is now obvious. You claim you knew nothing of the will, but that's a verbal assertion opposed by a host of weighty and incontrovertible evidence gathered during the course of this investigation."

I couldn't recollect myself for the shock of it: how and why had Pavel Alexandrovich made out a will in my favour? I focused on this question for a few moments and was suddenly struck by a possible explanation for it all. However, I did not mention this to the investigator.

"I should like to know," he continued, "what you have to say to this."

"First of all, that it would be odd, to say the least, if it were true that I had acted as the investigation, not without a certain logic, seeks to establish. What could be more foolish and naive than the behaviour of such a murderer? He knows he cannot conceal the fact of his visit to Shcherbakov, that what he stands to benefit from the death of this man is indisputable and all too apparent, and that suspicion in the first instance will fall on him. Yet there he goes one evening to Shcherbakov's, not by chance, but by invitation, kills him, returns home and fancies that if anyone were to ask him about it he'd simply say he didn't kill anyone and that he would naturally be believed. You must admit that only a man whose mental faculties ought to be the subject of clinical study could act in such a way."

Everything the investigator said to me and everything I said in response was marked by a peculiar clarity and precision—to which I was now quite unaccustomed, having lost it long ago.

"There's almost always a clinical element," said the investigator, "in the logic of every murderer; criminal reports continue to substantiate this. Herein lies the difference between their logic and that of normal people, and this is the Achilles' heel, so to speak, of any murderer."

"Yes, yes, I understand. There's always a certain pathological moment," I said. "It usually manifests itself as some minor miscalculation. But such sheer stupidity in the behaviour of a would-be murderer—doesn't that seem even more unlikely to you than this whole series of coincidences? For me this is a matter of life and death, and I intend to defend myself to the last. But I give you my word only to speak the truth."

His distant eyes looked at me as though he were thinking something I could never know. Then he said:

"I'm going to do something that is perhaps a little unorthodox. Let us suppose that you aren't the murderer, although, I repeat, the evidence is stacked against you. I admit, the arguments you have just presented had already occurred to me: it's much too obvious, and it's truly rather strange. Were it not for the fact that I've met and spoken to you, and had I just been told about this, I would have said that an investigation would be a waste of time. But I will try to help you. Do you remember what you and Shcherbakov were talking about on the night of his murder?"

Silence filled the large office. I was sitting in a chair, smoking a cigarette; to anyone else it might have looked as if two friends were having a quiet conversation about some abstract matter.

"Yes, yes," I replied. "I remember everything now. It all began when I mentioned how much I enjoyed watching the fire, finding something atavistic in this love for flames. My friend agreed with me; then we began to talk about death. He said that he often thought about it and found a certain comfort in these thoughts. He quoted from the Orthodox funeral rites and an obituary that might have appeared in the papers. I told him that death lacked any allure for me whatsoever. I recall it now as clear as day: I said to him that he had no heirs, no one to make a *will* for. Then came a few personal recollections that had no particular significance. One of the last things we discussed was Buddhism."

"If I understand correctly, then, the conversation meandered without any logical sequence to it," he said. "We would call it *une conversation à bâtons rompus*. But perhaps you're able to recall the link, the association that led you from personal anecdotes to a discussion of religious doctrine?"

"That's very simple," I replied. "Above Pavel Alexandrovich's head…"

"You mean to say, above the divan where he was sitting?"

"He was sitting on the armchair, not on the divan," I said. "The divan was to the right of the armchair, a little off to the side."

"You're quite right; my mistake. Please, do go on."

"Above his head was a bookshelf, and on this shelf stood a golden statuette of the Buddha."

"Can you describe it to me?"

"I'd recognize it among a thousand others."

"What was so unusual about it?"

I described the golden Buddha in detail and said that I was struck by its ecstatic face and the similarity of its expression to that of St Jerome.

The investigator's face suddenly tensed.

"That's odd," he said under his breath, more to himself than to me. "That's very odd. Did you imagine this statuette to be particularly valuable?"

"I'm no expert in such objects. For me its value was primarily aesthetic. However, I believe it must have been worth a great deal; it was made of solid gold, and there was a ruby set in it, albeit a very small one. In any case it was a remarkable statuette."

"Very well," he said. "So, you see the gold Buddha, and this naturally made you think of…"

"…of Buddhism and nirvana. Pavel Alexandrovich handed me the statuette so that I could examine it properly. While it was on the shelf, I hadn't been able to see it in all its glory: a lamp was shining on the table and the books were in the shadows."

"What did you do with the statuette next?"

"I handed it back to Pavel Alexandrovich, who placed it back on the shelf."

"You're sure of this?"

"Of what in particular?"

"That he put it back on the shelf."

"I'm certain."

"Very well," he said. "I'll have more questions for you later."

Back in my cell, I set my mind to work on the murder of Pavel Alexandrovich. Unlike my interrogators, I knew one vital detail—that I was not the murderer. The first hypothesis to enter my head was that Amar was the murderer. But I failed to see why he would do this. There could be no question of jealousy. Nor of any immediate advantage: Pavel Alexandrovich was supporting Lida, and Amar was living off the money she received. Moreover, the apartment had been left perfectly in order, there were no signs of any struggle, no attempt at theft, and everything was in its rightful place. Could it have been a man from the street, some random criminal? That seemed equally improbable—mainly because nothing had been stolen.

There was one other thing that seemed strange—the murder weapon. Pavel Alexandrovich had been killed with a knife to the back of the head, causing death instantaneously. At least, that is what I had managed to glean from the investigator. This, too, was a mystery. What type of knife could it have been? The instrument of death could not have been any ordinary broad-bladed knife. In any case, whatever the type of knife, the blow must have been delivered with exceptional strength and precision. It was unlikely that the ailing, consumptive Amar would have possessed such an unerring eye or the requisite physical strength. Moreover, for the hundredth time, why on earth would he have done it? The most likely remaining hypothesis—absurd as it was, it could not entirely be discounted—was that Pavel Alexandrovich had been the victim of some maniac.

When I was next brought in for questioning, I waited impatiently to hear what the investigator had to say. He sat down, laid a piece of paper in front of him and asked me in exactly the same tone, as if he were continuing an interrogation that had been interrupted only a few minutes ago:

"You say you remember the gold statuette of the Buddha in minute detail?"

"Yes."

"What was it standing on? Did it have a base of any sort?"

"No," I replied. "There was no base. The underside of the statuette was a perfect square, the one difference being that the corners were slightly rounded."

He handed me the sheet of white paper and asked:

"Is this the approximate shape of the underside?"

On the paper there was a faint line drawing of a perfect square with rounded corners.

"That's it exactly."

The investigator nodded. Then he looked me in the eyes and said:

"Whoever killed Shcherbakov must have taken the gold Buddha. There was a square imprint left on a shelf that was covered by a thin layer of dust. You're holding a tracing of it in your hands right now. If we can find the statuette, you'll be free to return home and continue your research on the Thirty Years War, the notes on which we found in your room. I must say, however, that I completely disagree with your conclusions, and in particular your appraisal of Richelieu."

He then handed me a cigarette—this silent gesture immediately said more than any alteration in the tone of his voice could have done. He did it almost automatically, as one might offer a cigarette to a friend. I felt a strange sense of relief, and my breathing quickened.

"Let's move on to another matter," he said. "What do you know about the deceased's mistress, her parents and her protector? I'd find it difficult to imagine that you haven't given any thought to the possibility of their having some part in the murder."

"I've given it a lot of thought," I said. "I've got a fair idea of the people we're dealing with, but least of all I know Amar, Lida's 'protector', as you call him. Not one of them is a respectable sort. Although I have to say, I fail to see how Lida or Amar could stand to profit by this murder."

"One could be forgiven for thinking that you're completely indifferent to the outcome of this investigation."

"My line of reasoning may differ somewhat from yours," I said, "but this is because I'm in possession of first-hand information that for you isn't proven *a priori*: I know I didn't kill Shcherbakov."

"At first glance, Lida and Amar appear to have a water-tight alibi," he said. "They both spent the night at L'Étoile d'Or, a dance hall. The waiters on both the first and second shifts remember Amar ordering champagne for them."

"It happened on a Saturday night, when there will have been a crowd. An hour's absence could easily go unnoticed."

"Yes, and what's more, we have reason enough to doubt any testimony from that lot. However, until we have proof to the contrary, we're obliged to go along with it."

"Still, I can't see what Amar could have been trying to achieve by killing Shcherbakov."

"Nor can we, and this stands in his favour. We searched their residence and questioned them, but to no avail. Lida's parents spent the night at home, and in any case I see no reason to suspect them. What are you able to tell me about them?"

I told him what I knew. He said:

"Of course, that speaks volumes for their character, but frankly it doesn't prove that either of them committed this murder, which has only left them out of pocket.

We have to find this statuette; it's the key to everything. I shan't pretend that finding it will be an easy task. I see no reason to question you any further. Now you must wait; time is on your side."

Before sending me away, he added:

"If the murderer hadn't been tempted by the golden Buddha, you'd be facing the guillotine or a lifetime's hard labour. I doubt whether the knowledge that the annals of justice would have been enriched by yet another case of a man being convicted for a crime he didn't commit would have been any consolation to you."

I couldn't even begin to imagine how long I would have to wait. But at least I was now certain that I was out of harm's way. True, I had imagined that the investigator, now being convinced of my non-implication in Shcherbakov's murder, might have restored me to freedom; however, placing myself in his shoes, I fancied that I should have acted in much the same way, if only so that Pavel Alexandrovich's real murderer would continue believing himself to be out of danger. As I subsequently found out, this was indeed the case to a certain degree. It later occurred to me that in the realm of elementary logic every individual reasons in much the same way, and it is ultimately the arbitrary laws of this peculiar branch of mathematics that leads to the arrest of a killer or to a crime's solution—especially as criminals are so often primitive people, incapable of any abstract thought, and

GAITO GAZDANOV

in this sense are defenceless against the slightest intellectual advantage of even a middling investigator. This ought to be a case in point, I thought.

I never gave any thought to the likely duration of my incarceration, nor did I keep track of the time I spent there; in spite of this, I was unconsciously prepared to believe that it might last for a couple of days. However, several weeks elapsed with no change in my circumstances. Sometimes it began to seem as if years could go by like this—not because I ought to have remained in custody, but because I was but one man among a crowd of millions in Paris and I had somehow found myself arrested, facing the prospect that I could simply vanish and be forgotten. This, however, was neither conjecture nor deduction, but a dark, vague presentiment; it was yet another obvious fault in my muscles, my vision, my hearing, my whole imperfect sensory apparatus. Days went by. At first I was unable to think about anything, but then I began to remember a whole array of things that were entirely unconnected with the murder. I always had to make such an effort to force myself to consider what it was that had played the chief part in my fate. It struck me that Pavel Alexandrovich's tragic and untimely death had failed to stir in me any pity or sorrow, feelings that I should have been experiencing and that would have been only natural. A strange sensation suddenly took hold of me—I myself found it difficult to put my finger on—as if everything had essentially been set in motion the moment it was revealed that Pavel Alexandrovich was no longer of this world. He had unsuspectingly, and now as though for ever, acquired that haunting, picturesque quality that had so struck me on the day I first met him in the Jardin du Luxembourg. I remembered all our conversations, his peculiar geniality, but now they somehow failed to provoke in me any emotional—I could find no other word for it— response. It occurred to me that he had come into my life at a time when everything was illusory and hypothetical, when the trees in the Jardin du Luxembourg had been no more real to me than the imaginary scenery in that far-off country I had never known. And yet what had taken place corresponded exactly with what I had been thinking about as I stood on that bridge across the Seine, on my way home from his apartment on the night of his death. Perhaps the very thought had coincided with the precise moment he died in that armchair, robbed even of the time to realize, perceive or comprehend that this was the journey into the other world that he had described to me in such lyric tones. This was the real crime—as it is with almost every murder: he had been deprived of what he had only begun to anticipate, the purpose of his long journey, a slow and gradual withdrawal from everything, the approach of nirvana, as he might have said during one of our conversations that was never to take place. And so it now struck me that I had been wrong in thinking it would have been better for him to die before he stopped appreciating his newfound happiness: I had arbitrarily dispossessed him of the single most important period in his life. I had stolen—and my only consolation was that it remained purely in the realm of theory—his right to a natural death, which had belonged to him, and to no one else. But time had not been on his side—and who could have known that there would be no journey, no approach of nirvana, but a quick gasp and instant darkness? Who could have known that there would be no obituary, no "bosom of Abraham, Isaac and Jacob", but the rigid body of an old man lying in a dissecting room before an autopsy, the very same body that Lida had held in her limp embrace the previous evening, as she closed her eyes and thought of Amar?

I noticed in my current condition a single attribute that could perhaps have been linked to the fact of my incarceration: whenever I began to think about something, I would find it more difficult than ever before to transfer my attention to something else. Normally I would have done this almost automatically: now, however, the images that used to fill my imagination seemed to have lost their former lightness and, more importantly, they had stopped submitting to my will, on which their appearance and disappearance no longer depended. Perhaps this was the effect of exhaustion. I tried to fight it as much as I could, but evidently I had little remaining strength. The moment finally came when I grasped the impossibility of distancing myself from what had long been approaching, from what I had tried to repress once and for all, because I knew nothing more painful or tragic. It began with three lines that haunted me:

> *But come you back when all the flow'rs are dying,*
> *If I am dead—as dead I well may be—*
> *You'll come and find the place where I am lying...*

Just then I heard the voice that had sung these words, a voice I had not heard for two years. Both the voice and these words emerged out of a sense of regret and loss, reminding me of my wilful and senseless rejection of the only chance I had to turn back the clock. How could I have thought then that I was unworthy of all this—the summer evenings, the intimacy with Catherine, her voice, her eyes and her diaphanous love? And how was it that these shadowy images, these descents into oblivion, my own shifting silhouette and the swaying instability of my life could seem so overwhelming that, fearing the inescapable illusoriness of existence, I would step into this abstract darkness, leaving that voice and these words behind, on the other side of this hateful expanse? Why did I do it? No one could have known for sure that I would have lost the battle. Had I really lacked the imagination to construct a seductive fictional reality? Would I really have been too weak to embody the image that Catherine had vaguely glimpsed, the one she had forgotten, the one she had invoked?

But come you back…

And so I closed the door behind me in order to dissolve slowly in her troubled sleep, in her fading memory. She was absolutely innocent; it was not she who had left me. I had stepped out of her room late one evening, and I recalled how slowly I had walked down those stairs. Only now did the absurdity of this slow motion reveal itself to me—because it had not been a departure, but very nearly a suicide; it had been a jump into the unknown.

For the first time in my life I felt as if I needed her help and support. It occurred to me that she might have heard something about the incident. Had she imagined that now, accused of murder and tormented by regret, I was waiting to learn of my fate and what awaited me— the guillotine, a lifetime of hard labour, or perhaps the return of the golden Buddha with its ecstatic face, and then freedom? Whatever the case, our relationship was nothing more than an illusion. Perhaps I would change, and in several years' time a remote convict, suffering terribly from malaria, would relate in that wretched criminal jargon the fantastic story of his love for this woman, whose existence would be believed by no one. But if by some miracle I were destined ever to meet her again, I would tell her—as always, half in English, half in French—about my interrogation, my standing accused of murder and my incarceration in prison. And I would add that it had been then, as I sat there, locked within these four walls, that I finally grasped the most important thing of all: that the constant spectre of someone else's existence, the accusation of murder, the remorse for being theoretically culpable before the shadow of my deceased friend, the prison, the prospect of a slow or instantaneous death—all this was far easier to bear than the memory of my departure from her room late that evening, than the disappearance of the only illusion for which, perhaps, it was truly worth defending myself to the bitter end.

*   *   *

I knew that over the course of these long days—which seemed to be filled with only my thoughts and memories, and which so monotonously transformed first into dusk and then into night—there, beyond the walls that confined my current existence, tireless work was being done. I concocted dozens of hypotheses, but of course I was unable to imagine even in the remotest, most abstract way possible what it would ultimately be that effected my return to freedom. Indeed I had no way of knowing that Thomas Wilkins was in Paris, much as I had no idea that he existed at all or that it would fall to him to play such a significant role in my fate, which was in turn the result of certain character traits of his. Thomas Wilkins was the owner of a large flower shop in Chicago, and, as he himself said, he loved two things above all else: flowers and women. Those who knew him best, however, were inclined to say that his greatest weakness was in fact for spirits. He had come to Paris on business, installed himself in the Grands Boulevards and soon became a regular in all the bars in the area. He was a stout forty-year-old man with faded eyes, and would usually turn up accompanied by a young lady who would rank among those well known to all the waiters and proprietors of those bars. He was renowned for a certain forgetfulness when under the influence of spirits, and on departing would often leave behind at the bar a box of chocolates, a parcel or even his own hat. These would usually be returned to him the following day.

The search for the golden Buddha had been entrusted to an Inspector Prunier, who, after spending a number of weeks on the case, was unable to uncover not only the whereabouts of the statuette, but even the slightest mention of it. He searched—albeit not without difficulty—the premises of the antiques dealer, who confirmed the sale of the Buddha to Shcherbakov several months previously; his corroboration, however, did nothing to advance matters. He provided Prunier with a detailed description of the statuette, which corresponded exactly with the one I had given to the investigator, and, thus having ascertained that the golden Buddha did indeed exist and was not a figment of my imagination, Prunier once again took to his searches. By the most elaborate and indirect of means he made enquiries with all the buyers of stolen goods, but they yielded no results. The golden statuette of the Buddha seemed to have vanished without trace.

Late one evening, as he was returning home, tired and sleepy, along one of the little streets near Place de l'Opéra, he stopped in front of a bar above which glowed a red neon sign. Muffled music could be heard coming from within. He pushed open the glass door and stepped inside. The place was nearly empty. He sat down on a bar stool opposite the cashier, greeted him—he knew all the staff there—ordered himself a grape juice and spotted to the right of the cashier a small object wrapped in crumpled tissue paper.

I learnt these details from Prunier himself, with whom I later became acquainted after inviting him to lunch at a restaurant. He related to me in vivid detail everything that had happened, the particulars of each interrogation and the trail of evidence that had led the investigation to its logical conclusion. Having had too much to drink, he was utterly candid and admitted to me that he was dissatisfied with his job and his lot, that he was compelled to do this work only because of a lack of sufficient means, and that what interested him more than anything in the world was zoology. When he started talking about this he became uncommonly animated, and it was impossible to stop him. I fancied that if a question on the classification of mammals had come up at the start of our conversation, I would scarcely have managed to find out anything at all about matters that in this instance were more pertinent to me personally, but to which he was little inclined to ascribe any importance. He went into a veritable lyric ecstasy when he began on Australian fauna, of which he possessed a surprising knowledge: he described to me the behaviour of the viper, the temperament of the platypus, the ferociousness of the dingo and the tragic beauty—as he phrased it—of the black swan. He knew the dimensions of the Manchurian tiger, the colours of the ocelot, the extraordinary speed of the hyena—he apparently felt unhindered by the fact that I was manifestly ignorant in this area. After this we met frequently; he was a kind man and carried within him the seed of a distinct zoological poetry, which was imbued, as I once remarked to him, with a sort of elemental pantheism. Luckily, however, that evening in the bar, his thoughts were far from zoology. He looked at the package and asked:

"What have we here?"

"A customer forgot it," said the cashier. "He only just left, I haven't had time to see what it is. Something heavy, in any case."

"Let me see it," said Prunier.

The cashier handed him the near formless package whose shape was concealed by several layers of paper. Prunier unwrapped the crumpled layers of tissue paper, and his eyes opened wide: there, glittering dimly in the electric light, was the ecstatic golden face of the Buddha peering up at him.

"*Ça, par exemple!*"* he said.

Wilkins was questioned the following day with the aid of an interpreter—he spoke almost no French. At first he was reluctant to talk to the police, insisting that he was an American citizen, that he had committed no crime, and that he had contacted the American consul, requesting his protection from the tyranny of the French authorities. However, once the matter had been explained to him, he told them what little he could. He had bought the statuette for three hundred francs from the girl with whom he had spent the previous evening. He had been very taken with its unusual lively expression, as he put it, and for that reason he had decided to acquire it, although naturally it was not worth such a sum, as it was made of bronze, with an inset piece of red glass. The girl initially had no intention of selling it and had only agreed to it after he insisted. She was a very lovely blonde, and was called Georgette. Prunier thanked him for his statement and asked at the bar who exactly this woman was who had arrived with Wilkins that evening.

* Well I never!

"Gaby," said the barman.

Half an hour later, Gaby was standing in front of Prunier. She began by declaring that all her documents were in order, that she would say nothing, that she had nothing to say, and that she knew her rights.

"Cut it," said Prunier. "And don't waste my time. Where did you get that statuette?"

"It was a gift."

"Very well. Who gave it to you?"

"That's none of your business."

"Oh, but it is," he said. "Well?"

"I'm saying nothing."

"As you wish," said Prunier. "But I'll have to detain you for having been complicit in the receipt of stolen goods."

"You must be joking," said Gaby. "Who would steal a bronze statuette?"

"A person who can tell the difference between bronze and gold. Well?"

This remark made a peculiarly strong impression on Gaby. Tears welled in her eyes; she couldn't forgive herself for having given away, practically gratis, such a precious object to this American who had been blind drunk, or at least made himself out to be so, and who also had no idea that it was gold.

"Gugusse told me it was worthless."

"You may go," said Prunier. "Just be sure not to go far, I may need you again."

After this, Gugusse, Gaby's official pimp, was delivered to that same room where Gaby had been only an hour ago. Prunier threw a sharp glance at him; Gugusse looked as he always did—his voluminous curls, the fruit of the hairdresser's labours, that sinister shaven face, and the light-brown suit with the grey overcoat.

"Good afternoon, Inspector," he said.

"Good afternoon, Gugusse," said Prunier. "How are things?"

"So-so, Inspector."

"Would you care for a cigarette?"

Such unexpected courtesy from the police inspector rather unnerved Gugusse; he was used to being addressed in quite a different manner, and this change in tenor betokened nothing good.

"You've always been a good lad at heart," said Prunier. "Of course, you've had a few run-ins, but then who hasn't?"

"Quite so, Inspector."

"There you go. You know, we do all we can not to make any unpleasantness for you: you live as you please, work as you please, and we don't inhibit you, because we're convinced of your integrity."

Prunier stared intently at him. Gugusse avoided his gaze.

"On the other hand, you must understand that since we're doing you a service, we're also counting on your loyalty. We know that if we were to require certain information, you'd give it to us. Is that not so?"

"Certainly, Inspector."

"Where did you get the statuette you gave to Gaby?"

"I don't know what you're talking about, Inspector."

"Alas, you see, it's impossible to have complete trust in you. A pity. For you must understand, of course, that everything will go well only so long as we believe you. But it wouldn't be difficult if all of a sudden we wanted to find something on you. There would be questions—and you know what that means—your past would be subjected to scrutiny—you know what that means too—and so on. Do you follow me? And then I'd no longer be able to protect you. I'd say, 'Gugusse, my hands are tied, because you abused my trust.' I hope you understand this. Now permit me to add that time is not something I have in abundance. For the last time: where did you get that statuette?"

"I found it in a rubbish bin, Inspector."

"Fine," said Prunier, standing up. "I see you've grown tired of the quiet life. Well then, there's more than one way to skin a cat."

"Amar gave it to me for safekeeping, Inspector."

"That's another matter entirely. You know, only recently we were talking about you, and I said to my colleagues, 'Chaps, I'm always ready to vouch for Gugusse.' I'm so glad I was right to say so. When did he give it to you?"

"In the early hours of the twelfth of February, Inspector."

*   *   *

Having been left alone with my thoughts, I knew nothing of these events at the time. I imagined that my fate would be decided presently, in these very days, and that nothing would depend on me in any way at all. Less than at any other time in my life was everything that lay before me defined by what I was or what I sought to be. I later returned to these thoughts and again established that they were truly insignificant. What was important was that there was a golden statuette with a square base, that the old antiques dealer with his spectacles and yarmulke had provided a detailed description of it to the police inspector, that Thomas Wilkins, the owner of that flower shop in Chicago, had a weakness for spirits and the fairer sex, and a tendency towards forgetfulness when drunk. What was important was the existence of Gaby, and that she worked in the Grands Boulevards. What was also important was that amid this unlikely pattern of drunkenness, flowers, prostituted women's bodies and semi-literate *souteneurs* there had appeared this golden incarnation of a great sage, of whose teachings not one of its temporary owners—not Wilkins, not Gaby, not Gugusse—knew the first thing, yet whose physical restitution held the key to my freedom. Besides, what other than the blind, inexorable workings of chance could have connected my fate, my delirium, my wanderings to the clientele of a flower shop in an

American metropolis—a clientele whose very existence had enabled Wilkins to make his journey to Paris? What could have linked it to Gaby and Gugusse's poorly treated syphilis and to the mysterious life of this Hindu artist to whose undeniable, and to some extent seditious, art the golden Buddha owed its existence? Perhaps this unknown master, as he worked on the statuette, had hoped that a hundred or a thousand years thence, having been resurrected and reincarnated dozens and dozens of times over, he would finally attain perfection and come to resemble that great sage of every age and nation—instead of dying, only to awaken as a pariah surrounded by spirits of darkness, having led an ordinary human existence, undistinguished by any particular service. It occurred to me that I had been far from the truth in telling Pavel Alexandrovich that under certain conditions I could become a Buddhist, precisely because my fate in this life interested me too much and I was anxious to regain my freedom.

The great day finally came three weeks later. Once again I was escorted to the investigator's office. He greeted me—which he had never done before—and said:

"I wasn't under any obligation to summon you, but I wanted to see you again and I had the time to spare."

He opened his briefcase—and the next thing I knew, I saw the golden Buddha in his hands.

"Here is your saviour," he said. "He did, however, prove rather difficult to find."

He carefully examined the statuette.

"It's a remarkable object," he said, "although I'm unable to find in it any resemblance to St Jerome, and I suspect your comparison to have been an exceedingly arbitrary one. Exactly which painting did you have in mind?"

"I'll admit I'm no connoisseur of paintings," I said. "I was reminded of an anonymous painting that caught my attention in the Louvre. It was attributed, unless I'm much mistaken, to the school of Signorelli. The painting seemed to be the work of two artists, and it depicts St Jerome in religious ecstasy. He's holding a stone to his bare chest, and blood is trickling down from under it. His face is raised to the heavens, his eyes are rolled back in a sacred frenzy, the lips on his aged mouth have almost disappeared; floating in the air, above his head, there is a vision of the Crucifixion. I thought it to be the work of two artists because the floating Crucifixion is executed carelessly and unconvincingly in comparison with the powerful expression inscribed in St Jerome's face by the artist. The statuette struck me primarily because of its expression of ecstasy, which seemed so unexpected on the face of the Buddha, as in every other portrayal that I've seen his face expresses an Olympian calm."

"I hope we shall have the opportunity to discuss this further at some point," he said. "Tonight you shall sleep in your own bed. Amar has not yet been arrested, but of course it's only a matter of time."

"Has the order for my release already been signed?" I asked. "What I mean to say is, may I now speak to you as a free man?"

"Of course."

I then told him my impressions of Amar and repeated that I personally doubted Amar's ability to deliver such a strong and precise blow.

"I've seen him," I said. "He's physically frail, weakened by illness. You just have to look at the way he walks to be sure of this—he limps."

"This point struck me as odd, too, to begin with," he replied. "But I've since had the occasion to consider evidence that was naturally unavailable to you."

"Namely?"

"The results of the post-mortem, for one. And also the dossier on Amar."

"What did the post-mortem reveal?"

"That the weapon used was no ordinary knife, but one with a triple-edged blade—something like a bayonet. Of the sort used in abattoirs."

"You mean to say…"

"I mean to say that until he fell ill, Amar worked in an abattoir in Tunis."

"I see," I said. "Yes, this is the way it had to be."

* * *

Recalling this period later, I couldn't help but observe the pre-eminence of two things: a strange levity and the impression of having witnessed the disappearance of an entire world. This sense of freedom was new and rather alarming, although it seemed as if it could come to a halt at any moment and then again I would vanish from this reality, borne away by a surge of that irrational force that had played such a significant part in my life to date. Yet each time I discovered my fears to be unfounded, or in any case premature.

Lida came to visit me as soon as she learnt of my release. Her face bore the mark of tears and she kept sobbing whenever Pavel Alexandrovich's name was mentioned. According to her, she had had as little to do with the murder as I did; the very notion of such a monstrous occurrence was unthinkable. She hadn't the faintest idea about Amar's schemes; he had evidently acted out of uncontrollable jealousy. Her happiness—the happiness she had earned through the dragging years of that dismal life of hers—hadn't been long-lived. Why had she sent for Amar? She knew that I held an undeservedly low opinion of her, and she was ready to forgive me, because I, of course, had not had to endure the travails of her life, and was in no position to understand her motives, her desires, her love. She was ready to repent of her unwitting complicity as much was as necessary.

"Here I sit before you," she said, "completely broken

and destroyed. Fate has taken from me what little I had, and now I am left with nothing. I ask you, what am I to do? Tell me, and I promise you I shall heed your every word."

I listened to her half-heartedly, curious to know who or what had put these words in her mouth. If this was her own initiative, then it proved yet again that she was cleverer than one might have been led to expect.

"I fail to see why you should need my advice," I said. "You've got by without it thus far. You speak as though you and I are bound by some mutual obligation, which has no basis in fact."

"Are you insinuating that you and I aren't in any way bound by this? You were Pavel Alexandrovich's friend and I am the woman he loved. Don't you think his memory in any way obligates you?"

"Forgive me, but I don't quite understand what you're getting at."

She raised her heavy eyes to meet my gaze.

"You once told me, in answer to what I said about our belonging to different worlds—which you didn't very much like—that everything in your world was different from mine. In other words, I thought that if in the world to which I have the pleasure of belonging I'm unable to count on anything other than spite, avarice and bestial emotions, then at least I might have been within my right to expect something better from yours: compassion, understanding, some movement of the soul that isn't dictated by selfish considerations."

I looked at her in sheer amazement. Who had taught her to speak and to think like this?

"I see now how very little I knew about you," I said. "In fact, only what you deemed it necessary to reveal to me. But never had I imagined I would hear words like that from Amar's lover. Wherever did you learn to do it?"

"You weren't listening very attentively when I told you the story of my life. For several years I worked for an old doctor who had a large library; I read a lot of books."

"And he died of natural causes?"

She shot me a look of reproach. I said nothing. Then she said:

"Apparently your world has the potential to be even crueller than mine. Yes, he died of natural causes."

"The very thing that Fate, as you call it, denied to Pavel Alexandrovich."

"It was a double murder. Because ever since he died I, too, have felt as though I've ceased to exist."

I experienced a complex emotion as I listened to these words of hers—fury, disgust and pity.

"Listen," I said, trying to remain calm, although it required great effort. "I'll tell you what I think. You chose to throw your fate in with Amar's."

"I loved him," she said in a listless voice.

"It wasn't in vain that you went to Africa. You'll have seen cesspits in the blazing sunlight. You'll have seen the little white maggots slowly crawling about in the filth beneath them. There's probably some biological reason for their existence, but I can picture no more revolting a spectacle. Every time I think about Amar I see it, and I have to stop myself retching. You claim your love for him plunged you into this filth, but no power on earth, no readiness to follow anyone's advice, no water will wash you clean of this. Allow me to be utterly frank. Just as they rent out rooms in hotels, so too did you rent out your body—and you ought to thank me for not using a more accurate phrase—to Pavel Alexandrovich. Even you have to admit that it wasn't worth the price he paid for it."

She stared at me unflinchingly with her heavy gaze. I gulped and found it difficult to speak.

"And now you come to me for advice. Though your intentions are too transparent for me to doubt them. The very thought of being touched by you disgusts me."

"Is that so?" she said, rising to her feet. I stood up from the chair where I was sitting. Her pale and somehow genuinely terrifying face—it was no accident that she was the lover of a murderer—came towards me.

"Get out!" I said almost in a whisper, because my voice cracked. "Get out, or I'll strangle you."

She burst into tears, buried her face in her hands and left the room. I felt remorse and pity—too late and in vain—essentially because I knew that nothing could be put right, nothing could be regained. Her behaviour and calculations had been at once both natural and incorrect. With an intellect such as hers, she ought to have understood that in acting like this she was bound to make a false move. Nevertheless, she was the victim of the milieu in which she had spent her life, of the memories that weighed heavily on her, of the combination of black and sorrowful things that made up her existence. No books could alter this. Naturally it would have been unfair to condemn her for failing to resemble the heroine of some virtuous novel, but she was what she was, and this had been the cause of everything, right down to her choice of lover and her devotion to him. I, on the other hand, could never believe that she had known nothing of the murder plan, although I was sure that she would never tell anyone. So, in order to find out, I would have to wait for Amar's arrest and confession.

When they came for him he had already fled, vanishing seemingly without trace, just as the golden statuette of the Buddha had done not so long before. Prunier fancied he might have returned to Tunis. In any case, days went by and the police were unable not only to find Amar, but even to uncover any trace of him where they looked. Nevertheless, the investigator had known what he was saying when he told me that his arrest was only a matter of time. Sooner or later some friend or acquaintance to whom Amar had given a sharp rejoinder, who envied his prosperity in Paris, or who wanted to indemnify himself with the police, just on the off chance—for whatever the reason, perhaps insignificant at first glance, the relevant person would eventually be informed that Amar was hiding in a certain location or could be found at a particular café. It might be in Paris, Nice, Lyons, or even in Tunis, but it was inevitable nevertheless. He might have made the crossing to South America—but he probably lacked the necessary funds for this, and it was unlikely that he had considered the option. As it turned out, he had stayed awhile in Marseilles, before returning to Paris.

He was discovered in one of the cafés near Place d'Italie, whereupon he made a run for it. Later several newspapers carried descriptions of the circumstances of his arrest, dubbing him a coward. I thought this unfair. Of course he lacked moral fibre, as it emerged under interrogation and later during the trial. But he possessed undoubted physical bravery. He was slow to understand what was happening to him, if indeed he understood it at all; a violent and primitive man, he was barely able to read and write. Neither his spiritual fortitude nor his mental faculties would ever have permitted him to comprehend the necessity or possibility of defending himself, even if it were to have dawned on him that his position was hopeless. He was incapable of understanding that there could be some other reality apart from the one that was defined by the most elementary ratio of physical forces. Yet he had the bravery of a hunted animal that was defending itself. Everything about his behaviour evidenced that he was incapable of understanding the situation: had he been able to comprehend it—which was not a difficult task—he would have surrendered without attempting to resist arrest. He was pursued by two police officers. What could he have hoped to achieve by running? He had a limp, and so it was obvious that he wouldn't get far. He was ultimately thwarted by a miscalculation in his escape route: he headed down a blind alley, believing it to be a street. When the first policeman caught up, Amar pulled a knife on him—the most dangerous weapon he was carrying, which he handled like a virtuoso. It turned out, however, that this policeman was a more than a match for any adversary armed with a knife, and he managed very quickly to shield himself from the attack with his navy-blue cloak. Had he moved a fraction of a second later, he would have been killed. By now, the second policeman had managed to catch up, and he toppled Amar with a blow to the chin. It was all over in thirty seconds—and so a photograph of the arrested man was splashed across the evening papers.

His resolve not to answer any questions was quickly crushed, and he confessed to everything that had happened without sparing a single detail.

According to him, it had all begun with Zina's advice to her daughter that she ought to suggest to

Pavel Alexandrovich that he make a will. For a while, Shcherbakov avoided discussing the matter, but then one day he announced that the will had been drawn up and was in the care of a notary. Naturally, not Zina, not the mousey marksman, not Amar himself and not even Lida had any doubt at all that Pavel Alexandrovich would leave everything to her: how else could it have been? Then began a series of long and almost daily discussions of how exactly to get rid of him. While awaiting the final decision, Amar, acting on Zina's advice, began to take driving lessons—upon receipt of his portion of the inheritance he intended to buy himself a motor car. They all cultivated this exaggerated idea of Pavel Alexandrovich's wealth and were convinced he was a multimillionaire. Zina's lover suggested that they gradually poison him with arsenic. Zina thought it better to leave the gas tap on while he was asleep. Lida had no suggestions of her own, and while she made no objection to any of these stratagems, she remained very reticent on the subject.

Not one of these methods, however, met with unanimous approval, and so no decision was taken. They would just have to wait. But Amar wanted to own a motor car, he wanted to have at his disposal the money he would receive after Shcherbakov's death, and so he decided he could wait no longer. This is why he took it upon himself to put his own plan into action. At first glance the conditions seemed favourable. He knew I would be at Pavel

Alexandrovich's that evening, and although he had never seen me, yet he had a fair idea of what I looked like, and Lida had even said to him one day:

"This guy might be dangerous."

On the face of it Amar's calculation seemed remarkably simple and seductive, but his imagination extended no farther than the most immediate of considerations. The evidence was stacked against me. It never occurred to him to put himself in my shoes or to imagine what I might have done if I really were to have had the monstrous and senseless intention of murdering Pavel Alexandrovich. He believed his plan to be infallible. At the dance hall, while Lida was dancing with one of her many admirers, he stole the keys to Shcherbakov's apartment from her handbag and slipped them into his pocket. He told her that he was just going out for a moment and would be back soon; he stepped out into the street, hailed a taxi and took it as far as the corner of Rue Chardon-Lagache and Rue Molitor. It was almost one o'clock in the morning. Then he waited for me to leave.

"A few minutes later," he told the investigator, "I saw him leave the building. He stood there for a while, looked about and started walking down towards Rue Chardon-Lagache with his hands in his pockets. I waited another quarter of an hour, then I opened the door with the key and went in."

Pavel Alexandrovich had been asleep in his armchair and had heard nothing. On tiptoes Amar crept up behind him and thrust the knife into the back of his neck. Death was instantaneous. He wiped the blood from the knife with a handkerchief, and it was then that he noticed the golden statuette of the Buddha. He picked it up in order to examine it more closely and, without thinking, slipped it into his pocket. Then he left, locking the door behind him.

Everything was quiet, not a soul was around. On reaching the Seine, he wrapped the knife in the bloody handkerchief, tied a knot around it and cast it into the river. He then crossed over to the other bank and hailed another taxi, which he took almost as far as the corner of the street where the dance hall was located. There he met Gugusse, to whom he gave the statuette, asking him to keep hold of it for a short while. Then he returned to the dance hall. The orchestra was still playing, and Lida, as before, was still dancing.

"It was as if nothing had happened," he said.

He replaced the key in Lida's handbag and she, once the dance had finished, walked over to their table and asked Amar where he had been. He replied:

"You can thank me later. It's done."

But when he revealed to her a little later exactly how it had been done, she, according to Amar, flew into a rage. She told him that he had acted like an absolute fool, that he would ruin them all, that I would doubtless be able to prove that I had no part in the murder, and that both the inspector and the investigator would not treat me as they would treat him. After this Amar made a fatal error: he concealed from Lida the fact that he had stolen the statuette of the Buddha.

Lida's testimony fundamentally differed from Amar's version of events: she had known nothing of the murder until it was officially discovered by the maid who came to Shcherbakov's every morning, when she opened the door—she had a key to the apartment—to find Pavel Alexandrovich's corpse, which she immediately reported to the police. Lida and her family had never discussed any murder plans; the conversations that Amar mentioned had obviously been meant in jest: both Lida and her parents were on excellent terms with Shcherbakov and less than anyone would have wanted him dead. Pavel Alexandrovich himself had broached the need to make a will, but only because he had a weak heart and it was prudent to do so. She had been unable to inform the police that Amar was the murderer because he had threatened also to kill her if she breathed so much as a word of it to anyone.

I learnt all these details from various newspaper articles; confronted by the tragic events that had put an end to Pavel Alexandrovich's life, as well as those that had effected my release and material well-being—which had come about almost as unexpectedly as his—I became ever more convinced that Amar and Lida's fate, as with Pavel Alexandrovich's death, had been a part of some complex scheme that was not devoid of a certain ominous logic. After he was stripped, the police doctor noticed on his chest a tattoo which read: *"Enfant de Malheur"*.* Now he faced the guillotine or a lifetime's hard labour. That it was he who had committed this murder, which Lida had opposed not on principle but on solely technical grounds, was no accident. This was the final episode in his battle against the world to which he had been denied entry—because he was half-Arab, half-Pole, because he was barely literate, because he was poor, because he was consumptive, because he was a pimp, because there they spoke of things he did not know, in a language he did not understand. In any case, he had wanted to become a part of this world because it contained money, lavish apartments and motor cars—but most importantly, money. He was motivated not only by that, but by some vague understanding that another, better life awaited him there, one that could be accessed merely by stepping over the body of an old, defenceless man. Herein lay the error of his conceit—the desire to escape the living conditions in which he had been born and raised. He had naively supposed that in his hand he held the means by which to achieve his aim: a triple-edged knife. He had imagined that another man's late-night visit to the victim, much like the one that actually killed him, would mislead the investigator and everyone else. He had failed to grasp that he was as helpless as a child before these people, and that

* Child of Misfortune.

for his desperation and this illicit attempt to change the order of things he would pay with his own life. He was a condemned man even before the trial started, and his fate had long already been sealed, whatever the circumstances of his life. All this, of course, seemed to result from a string of coincidences: Tunis, meeting Lida, her acquaintance with Pavel Alexandrovich in Paris. Yet the inherent sense of these coincidences remained inalterable and would have been exactly the same even if they had been different. It would have changed nothing—or almost nothing.

He was on his own now. No one shared in his fate, and he could count on no help or compassion from any quarter. Lida would never support him, because she was too clever for that, and others—his friends—turned their backs on him, too, because they were essentially indifferent to his lot. Neither the investigator nor the people who tried him felt any hatred towards him, nor were they consumed by a thirst for revenge; he fell under such-and-such an article of the law, whose distant author, naturally, had no particular man in mind when he wrote it. And it seemed entirely inconsequential to everyone who had played a certain role in his fate that he, Amar, would presently cease to exist. Of course at first glance there was some easily demonstrable justice in all this—something of the same order as the peculiar logic that had led him to the guillotine. But this justice was far removed from the classical triumph of good over evil. No one had ever spent time explaining to Amar the difference between right and wrong, or the deepest intricacies of their connotations. If he had gathered anything from what was happening to him, it could only have been one thing: that he had made a mistake in his calculations. But for this, no consciousness of his guilt, nor any remorse for what he had done, would have tormented him. Pavel Alexandrovich's money would have been spent, and everything would have been just fine—until, that is, new evidence surfaced, leading him more or less back to his current position. However, it was more than likely that he would have died of consumption before this. He had the misfortune of belonging to that great mass of people—beyond his personal affiliation with the criminal world—whose interests every state lawmaker and almost every social and philosophical theory in existence would never fail to invoke; they provided material for statistical comparisons and conclusions, and it was in their name that revolutions had taken place and wars had been waged. But they were just that—material. Until then, while Amar had been working in the slaughterhouses of Tunis, covered in bloody, foul-smelling slime and earning in a month as much as his advocate would spend in Paris during the course of a single evening with his mistress, his existence had been economically and socially justified, although he had no knowledge of this. But since the day he stopped working he had become expendable. What could he say in his defence? In what way and to whom was his life necessary? He was no longer a unit of man-power, he was neither an office worker nor a bricklayer, neither an actor nor a painter, and so that tacit social law, uncodified but implacable, no longer recognized his moral right to live.

Even on the face of it he had been of absolutely no interest whatsoever until the moment he uttered that it was he who had killed Shcherbakov. In the wake of this admission a vacuum formed around him, and in this vacuum was death. Even the advocate defending him looked upon him only as a convenient pretext to practise his judicial rhetoric—because what ultimately did it matter to him, to this *maître* who lived in a comfortable apart-ment, to this young man who earned very well indeed, who took a bath daily, who had a loving and attentive wife, who read books by contemporary authors, who loved Giraudoux's plays and Bergson's philosophy—what did the fate of some dirty, consumptive Arab murderer mean to this distinguished gentleman, far removed from any such reality?

Now it was all over: he had been condemned to death and was awaiting the day when the sentence would be carried out. I recalled his terrible, dark face at the hearing, his black, dead eyes. Naturally he had been unable to follow what the prosecutor was saying, and so too with the defence; he understood only that he had been condemned to death. Listening first to the prosecutor's words, then to those of the defence, I was ready to shrug my shoulders and be done with it, so blatant was the artifice of their arguments. Yet it was, of course, inevitable—because in a judicial interpretation every element of a man's life is inevitably subjected to a fundamental distortion. The prosecutor said:

"We are not here to attack: we have come to defend ourselves. In passing sentence on the accused, we are defending those great principles upon which the existence of modern society and each and every human collective is based. I refer first and foremost to man's right to life. I should like this to be clear, and for there to be no doubt on this point.

"I reject outright the possibility of there being mitigating circumstances. I deeply regret their absence, for it will mean the death sentence, and if my conscience had permitted me not to insist on such a ruling I would have proceeded without hesitation to an analysis of these mitigating circumstances. Unfortunately, as I have just stated, there are none. It would be a dereliction of my duties if I failed to remind you that we are now judging a man who is culpable of two counts of murder. His first crime regrettably is irreversible. However, the man who would have been the accused's second victim escaped Shcherbakov's fate thanks only to the impeccable functioning of the judiciary, that same judiciary in whose name I am now addressing you. The accused's plan was constructed in such a way that suspicion was meant to fall on an innocent man, the deceased's closest friend, a young student who has his whole life ahead of him. If the accused's plan had been carried out as he intended, there would be in the dock right now a man whose death would be on your conscience. Thankfully that isn't the case. Although this man in no way owes his life and freedom to the magnanimity of the accused. With that same ruthless villainy he used to dispatch his first victim, he would have sent a second to the guillotine. It is for this reason that I stress this is a double murder. And so if his plight has stirred any pity in you, then just remember that you are perhaps saving several more lives with your good and impartial judgement.

"Let me now direct your attention to yet another point. In both these murders—one executed, the other meditated—never, not even for an instant, was there anything other than cold calculation. I'm the first to admit that not every instance of killing should automatically warrant the death sentence for the guilty party. There is manslaughter as the result of self-defence. There is revenge for outraged honour or insult. Before us lies a whole spectrum of human emotions, each one of which may lead to a tragic end. We would seek vainly to establish any such romantic motives in the murder committed by the man who appears before you. There is no way that this crime could have resulted from the relationship between the actors in this brief tragedy that you have been summoned to unravel. The accused did not know his victim personally, he had never seen him, nor could he have harboured any ill feeling towards him whatsoever. Any justification or explanation for this crime on grounds of personal or emotional motives—if one allows that personal motives may be a justification for such a crime—is altogether absent here. I shall not labour the heinousness of this crime: the facts are so articulate and persuasive as to render any commentary unnecessary. But I shall permit myself to point out the following: if in the first instance the murderer, a dull-witted and dubious character, was guided by interests of the basest and most material order, then in the second he was prepared to send to the scaffold or to hard labour a man whose disappearance would profit him not a single franc.

"It is not difficult to anticipate the defence's argument that the accusation of the second, attempted crime has no basis in fact. However, I repeat: that it did not take place should in no way be attributed to any sudden doubt or hesitation on the part of the accused. In returning repeatedly to this second crime, it is my intent to point out to you that the accused is no casual murderer. I beseech you: put an end to this series of murders. Stop it—for if you do not, and if in several years' time the accused is released, the death of his next victim will be on your conscience."

This was more or less what the prosecutor said; such was the basic argument of his case. I paid less attention to the part where he described exactly how the murder had been committed, unsparing of any detail and underscoring in every possible way the beastly, as he phrased it, savageness with which it had been carried out. When it came to Amar's life, he limited himself to noting that he had been tried several times in Tunis for theft and was, essentially, a professional pimp. The insistency with which he spoke of the second crime struck me as somewhat odd, and I was disposed to think that, while it was possible from a strictly legal perspective to accuse Amar of intending to obstruct the course of justice, he could not be accused of a murder that he had not premeditated, and ultimately had not committed. In any event, it was clear from the prosecutor's speech that the defendant himself was of no particular interest to him; he examined the case and established a psychological theorem, oversimplifying it to the extreme and reducing its solution to the briefest of formulas.

I doubt whether Amar would have been in any state to listen to this man who was sending him to the guillotine. But that was of no consequence, as even if he had caught every word he would still have been unable to understand. He understood only one thing, that he was being sent to his death, and this for him was the essential part—which came in contrast to the others, for whom what was important was exactly how and with what degree of oratorical persuasiveness, with which metaphors and expressions it would be done. The prosecutor mentioned Lida and her family only in passing: no formal accusations were brought against them, and he cautioned the court not to make the mistake of ascribing any exaggerated significance to the influence that the family had held over the defendant.

The real attack on Lida and her family, however, came from Amar's advocate. The prosecutor was a thin, sallow man, who looked as though he had been saturated with tobacco smoke and spoke in a high and surprisingly pathetic voice. He was extremely withered and resembled some ascetic image, temporarily and haphazardly personified in this emaciated human body. It seemed unimaginable that he could be capable of delivering a lyric monologue or of being naked with a woman in his embrace. The advocate had a naive, rosy face, a voice that was at once deep and sonorous, and to listen to him was less tedious that it was to listen to the prosecutor. His speech differed from the prosecutor's in that it was intended to work on a purely emotive level.

"Your Honour, gentlemen of the court," he said. "It seems to me that we must first try to avoid the temptation of crediting this simplistic interpretation of events, which, wittingly or unwittingly, the prosecution has drawn for us. I must immediately forewarn you that I am not in the possession of a single material argument that is capable of making my task any easier. I have at my disposal only the same material that was available to the prosecution, and there is not a single piece of evidence about which I would know and the opposing side would not. As you can see, I come unarmed. However, I should like to caution you against jumping to any premature conclusions that may seem logically sound but might lack the element of compassion and mercy that is also the very foundation of justice. And it is to uphold these basic tenets of justice that I now beseech you. But let us turn to the defendant and his two murders, about which the prosecutor so vehemently spoke. 'A dull-witted and dubious character,' the prosecutor called him. Yes, it was a dull-witted and dubious character who killed Shcherbakov and in so doing implicated another man, thus jeopardizing his life. You will agree that this second crime, in contrast to the first, was never actually committed, and, as we have been summoned here to examine only established facts, there can be nothing more incumbent upon us than to dismiss this accusation outright. However, I would go further still: the first crime, the first murder, also merits closer scrutiny. Was Amar the real murderer, or was he merely executing a criminal plan hatched by others—a plan that was never his own? Herein lies the most vital question.

"Compare the life story of this man with those of the others surrounding him. Amar was born and raised in poverty, he received no education, worked in the slaughter-houses of Tunis and led a poor and wretched life—that of the unfortunate natives of our African *départements*.

Who stirred in him the desire for another life, who had a taste for expensive restaurants, cabarets, the avenues of the Champs Élysées, night-time Paris, debauchery and extravagance, the transition from riches to poverty and from poverty to riches? Who advised Lida to urge for a will to be drawn up? Who discussed the various possibilities—not of killing, of course, but of getting rid of Shcherbakov? Who had need of his money? Compare Amar's testimony with Lida's and Zina's. He conceals nothing, he is incapable even of lying. You won't find a single tactical error in what either Lida or Zina has said. They knew nothing of the murder, they were devoted to Shcherbakov, they had only the most benevolent of feelings for him. Can you not see the scandalous, brazen duplicity in all this? To love a man—and to press for a will; to love a man—and to sleep in other men's beds; to love a man—and to spend whole evenings discussing in cold blood how most safely and conveniently to do away with him.

"There are other factors in this case, the exact significance of which remains unclear; however, their existence cannot be denied, and they cast doubt on the probability of that most simple and categorical interpretation advocated by the prosecution. In particular, the role of the young man on whom suspicion first fell and to whom Shcherbakov, for reasons completely unknown to us, left his entire fortune—the role of this student is murkier than it might at first seem. He had a fair idea of Lida and her mother's moral composition, and he knew of Amar's existence. Why then, as the deceased's closest friend, did he not warn him of the danger in such an association? What exactly did he mean by the mysterious answer he gave under questioning, when, denying that he was the murderer, he uttered the following mysterious words: 'It was just an arbitrary logical construct'? I do not contest his factual non-participation in the murder; to do so would be pointless after Amar's confession. Yet the fact alone that he considered it somehow logically permissible and, consequently, practicable seems most odd, and this, perhaps, warrants further investigation."

The entire defence was built around his original assertion, namely that Amar was only the instrument of someone else's criminal will, and that he ought to be judged as such. He laid all the blame on Zina and Lida, whose biographies he described in such rich detail, which attested to his extraordinary concern for the case. Evidently he approached his role of defence advocate exceedingly conscientiously, but it did not change the fact that Amar's fate interested him only insofar as it was linked to his success in the courtroom. He challenged every one of the prosecutor's arguments—with varying degrees of persuasiveness—but, in contrast to his opponent, he failed to devote enough attention to purely logical considerations, and this seemed to me to be his gravest error. He closed his speech with an appeal to the court, which turned out to be no less pathetic than the prosecutor's:

"The prosecution has called upon you to put an end to a series of murders, which, if we are to believe him, will inevitably follow on. If I may be so bold, I should like to state that cruel fate anticipated this eventuality well before the intervention of justice. You may rest assured: Amar will never pose a danger to anyone ever again. He is suffering from an acute form of tuberculosis, his lungs are haemorrhaging, and it would seem to me equally senseless and cruel if justice were to take on the woeful task that his illness has already resolved itself to do. By all accounts Amar has little time left to live: his days are numbered. And I appeal to you for mercy: allow him to die a natural death. The difference in time will be nominal, the difference in result will be nil. He is nevertheless condemned to death; do not take it upon yourselves to alter his inexorable fate. As I have just said, the result will be the same in any case. If you do not pass this sentence on him, you will have one fewer death on your conscience, and this man will die in a prison hospital, carrying with him the grateful memory that, although betrayed by his friends and the woman for whom he risked his own wretched life, he was shown mercy by those who saw him first in the dock, who were ultimately able to understand this dubious, poor Arab who paid for the crimes of others inciting him to kill."

The verdict was read after an hour's recess: Amar was sentenced to death. As I watched him, his lips quivered, he incoherently tried to say something, and a heavy shadow fell across his dark face. He saw that it was all over—and I thought then that the ghostly existence of those dead black eyes, that thin swarthy body with the tattoo on its chest, would continue for a short while, but only as an extended formality, and that this man was now essentially no different from those who had been killed on the battlefield, who had died from chronic illness, from the man who had been stabbed by a triple-edged blade and whose spectre had exacted such cruel revenge.

* * *

Returning home after several weeks' imprisonment, I was struck by the imperturbable constancy of everything I had lost on the day of my arrest and which I now regained. Those same people walked down that same street, those same acquaintances dined in those same restaurants; it was the same city and human landscape I had always known. Then with full force I perceived the sinister immutability of existence that was so typical of the people living in my street and that I had pondered that evening, which now seemed so infinitely distant, when I had stood by the window thinking about Michelangelo's *Last Judgement*. After I had restored order to the room and taken a shower,

I began to shave and looked at myself in the mirror; I was met again by that same, somehow inimical expression on my face. Those former thoughts returned to me with renewed strength, like a chronic headache, this constant searching, as persistent as it was fruitless, for some illusive and harmonious justification of life. I simply had to seek it out, because in contrast to those who held an almost rational belief in some divine beginning, I was inclined towards the notion that this insatiable desire to obtain something intangible could probably be attributed to some imperfection in my sensory organs; it seemed as indisputable to me as the laws of gravity or the Earth's spherical form. But although I had already been long aware of this, yet I could not stop thinking about it. When taking certain university courses and reading certain books directly relating to them I would subconsciously envy that professor or author to whom practically everything was clear and for whom the history of man represented an elegant series of events whose sole, incontrovertible purpose was to support the basic premises and conclusions of their political or social theories. There was something reassuring and idyllic about this, some metaphysical comfort that forever remained inaccessible to me.

It was a cold March evening; I donned my overcoat, left the apartment and went on a long walk through the streets, trying as best I could not to think about anything, apart from the approach of the capricious Parisian spring that was already in the air, the bright street lights and motor cars passing by, the absence now of prison, murder accusations and finally, for the first time in my life, the lack of material concerns for the future. I tried to instil in myself in as far as possible a consciousness of this undeniable good fortune of mine, and I kept listing, one after the other, the advantages of my current situation: freedom, health, money, the unimpeded ability to do whatever I wanted and go wherever I pleased. These were utterly indisputable; however, they were unfortunately just as indisputable as they were unreal. And again it began to seem as if I were gradually succumbing to that heavy, inexplicable sorrow, whose attacks could render me defenceless.

I was walking along one of the little quiet streets that lead onto Boulevard Raspail. On the ground floor of the building I was passing a window suddenly shot open and a phrase of music rang out amid the cold air, stopping me in my tracks—someone inside was playing the piano. I recognized the melody at once: the piece was called 'Souvenir', and I had first heard it several years ago, at a concert given by Kreisler. I had attended this concert at the Pleyel with Catherine; as she sat next to me, her misty tenderness had seemed to accentuate the sense of the melody, heightening the theme of memory in Kreisler's playing. Attempting to translate the movement of sounds into my poverty of words, the meaning was approximately thus: that the feeling of happy plenitude is short-lived and illusory, it will leave only regret and as such it is a sorrowful yet alluring warning. Because of this I knew that the moment could never be repeated, and I keenly sensed, perhaps because it too could never be repeated, the magic of the violin. This was the year that Catherine had arrived in Paris, to study; I had met her in a little restaurant in the Latin Quarter, where we ate every day and where a huge stove stood in the dining room among all the tables. There were gleaming red pots, a great many sauces spluttering away in their covered pans; it smelt of roasted meats and rich bouillon, and, over all this decorative brilliance of food and cuisine, as if transported here by some miracle from a Dutch painting, reigned an enormous, jolly proprietress, with saucy, gay eyes, raven hair, a high bosom, plump, shapely legs and an unforgettable contralto voice, which seemed almost to echo her Rubens-like power. "Do you remember her, Catherine?" I said aloud, immediately looking around, fearing that someone might have heard me. But there was no one. I continued on, thinking about what I would say to her if I were to meet her.

I would ask her whether she remembered the Kreisler concert. I would ask her whether she still remembered that warm April night as we walked through the streets of Paris and she told me, switching from English to French and from French back to English, about Melbourne, where she was born and raised, about Australia, about her first girlish love—a tenor in the opera, who before long had married a rich American—about the ships that came into dock, about the thunder of the anchor chains, about the golden-red lustre of the copper on the cruisers and torpedo boats in the sunlight. I would ask her whether she had forgotten the words she spoke to me back then. I would ask her whether she remembered the promise she made. I could hear every intonation in her voice:

"No matter where you are and when it happens, never forget: as soon as you feel strong enough, as soon as the clarity of your mind is no longer obscured, let me know. I'll drop everything and come to you."

I would tell her that I had thought of these words in prison, during those first days of my incarceration, when I still had no idea whether I would ever see freedom again.

I would tell her that her face had been distorted and unrecognizable as she had told me that she was with child, that it meant the end for her, that she could not allow it to happen, that there would be time later, that she was only twenty years old, with her whole life ahead of her. This, I am sure, she will never forget: the clinic walls daubed in white oil paint, the little female doctor of indeterminate nationality, her shifting eyes, the agonizing operation that was carried out without anaesthetic and the jolting of the taxi in which I had taken her home to the hotel room, her fainting fits during the journey and how I carried her from the taxi to her bed, how she had put her arms around my neck and how the vein at the back of her knee had quivered and pulsated. For two months after this I deprived myself of breakfast and lunch, living solely on bread and milk, while I paid off my debts to friends, as she and I had both lacked the money for the operation. That very evening, on the ground floor of the building opposite her hotel, there had been a wedding reception for the concierge's daughter, who had married some pimply youth in a dark suit, a junior clerk at a funeral parlour. The windows were wide open, and we could see a table decked with a wedding feast, the wooden face of the bride, frozen in an expression of joy, and the deep-crimson pimples of the bridegroom under the electric light. A motley group of relatives was sitting around the table, at times launching in unison into some offensively off-key musical trash. Their voices, however, grew ever more hoarse, diminishing and eventually dying away. Catherine fell asleep, and I spent the whole night sitting in an armchair at her bedside. In the morning, when she opened her eyes and saw me, she said:

"It's over now, it doesn't matter any more. You look very funny when you haven't shaved."

Later that day, as I succumbed to that strange illness I was powerless to resist, I told her about it and she looked at me, eyes wide with disbelief. I said that I had no right to tie her down with any sense of obligation, that I was ill and that if things had been different…

After that, whenever my mind journeyed back to her, I would force myself to think about something else. She moved out of the Latin Quarter, but I knew her new address: she was living on Rue de Courcelles, in a flat that belonged to an aunt of hers, who would come and go periodically but all the while kept the apartment on in perpetuity. Many times I had accompanied Catherine there, and many times I had waited for her in the street below.

I knew nothing of her new life, what she thought about and whether she recalled as well as I did that period of our existence. I had no idea whether her voice would tremble as she replied to my first words after all this time; I did not even know whether she would still be that same woman she had been at the Kreisler concert and in her hotel room—or whether in all that time she had spared a single thought for me. She would be twenty-three now, and of course it was unlikely that she had been awaiting my possible return all this time. Her promise belonged just as much to the past as did the life she had led three years ago, and I had no right to blame her if it were to turn out that she had been unable to keep it. This was obvious from the moment it crossed my mind. Yet it did not stop me, and the urge to make this desperate attempt to return to Catherine was much too overpowering to be hampered by such considerations. It seemed as if nothing could ever replace the great many feelings that welled within me whenever I thought about her or sensed her presence next to me. I essentially had nothing with which to counter this chaotic world, for everything I knew seemed limp and unpersuasive, or else incredibly distant, yet it was in this world that her existence came to me, like a unique embodiment of a mirage. Even her appearance reminded me occasionally, particularly in the evening or at dusk, of an ethereal spectre walking by my side. The light shone through her blonde hair, she had a pale face and pale lips, lustreless deep-blue eyes and the body of a fifteen-year-old girl. Her life, however, which so occupied my imagination, would outgrow this spectre and appear there, where everything seemed foreign and hostile to me.

Now, having acquired this double freedom—that of the body, leaving prison, and that of the soul, because the shock of it seemed to have cured me, perhaps once and for all—I felt surrounded by emptiness, and no one apart from Catherine seemed able to shelter me from this. I sought sanctuary in her; solitude and despair had made me weary, and I thought that now, for some reason at this very moment, I had earned the right to a different life. And so, as I walked home I resolved to go to Rue de Courcelles the very next day.

By ten o'clock the following morning I was there. I liked this part of Paris—the quiet streets and the tall dark buildings with their large windows, behind which trickled the steady flow of a measured life, where people thought in terms of incomes and shares in stocks, of suitors and inheritances; this was the stubborn nineteenth century, archaic and naive, whose slow death had already been dragging on for decades. In the building where Catherine's aunt lived there was an ancient lift operated by belts, and as I ascended to the third floor there was a slight hint of smoke, and I even had the impression that I saw a few sparks flying about in the smoke itself. I rang the bell; a plump woman with grey hair opened the door to me and asked what I wanted. Her French was fluent, although she spoke with an accent. I said that I had come to see Catherine.

"Catherine?" she repeated. "Catherine left for Australia a year ago."

"Ah yes, Australia…" I said automatically.

"She left just after her wedding."

"She got married?"

My voice must have betrayed a note of informality, although it was quite out of place in the presence of this woman whom I had never before met, for she said:

"Do come in and take a seat. I'm sorry, your name is…"

I introduced myself.

"Yes, yes. Catherine told me about you. Had you come a year ago you would have found her unattached."

"Yes, I understand," I said. "Alas, I've come a year too late."

She had a most peculiar and engaging smile—and I felt as if I had known this elderly woman for a long time. She looked me straight in the eyes and asked:

"Are you the lunatic?"

"Yes," I said, lost in my own thoughts. "That is to say, not quite. I'm not mad…"

"Forgive me," she said. "I'm a good deal older than you and, you know, I have a suspicion that you just dreamt the whole thing up. It's all because you read too much, eat too little and spare hardly any thought for the most important thing at your age: love."

I gathered from this that Catherine had told her a lot about me. I replied:

"I don't wish to appear rude, but that isn't a very scientific diagnosis."

"It may not be scientific, but I'm convinced of it nonetheless."

I momentarily fell silent. Then I asked:

"Whom did she marry?"

"An English painter. He painted this portrait," she said, raising her eyes to the wall. "His first wife, I believe."

The painting showed an improbable woman with a chocolate-box sort of beauty, wearing a red velvet dress; it looked like a bad oleograph. How had Catherine failed to see this?

I stood up and began to make my exit. She offered me her hand and asked me to leave my address, just in case.

The staircase was broad, with a heavy carpet laid over it; it looked nothing like the one in Catherine's hotel in the Latin Quarter. Yet all I could think of was this silent descent from the world she had once inhabited, back into the spectral abyss I had so struggled to escape.

*   *   *

Days, weeks and months went by. I left the Latin Quarter some while ago; throughout the streets of Paris, the trees had turned green, blossomed and then been covered in the dust of summer; then they shed their leaves and awaited the arrival of October. Amar was executed at dawn one cold morning. I read about it in the papers, where it was reported that he had downed a glass of rum and smoked a cigarette before mounting the scaffold. Once there he surveyed the people around him.

"*Du courage!*"* his advocate had said to him. Amar had wanted to say something, but couldn't get it out; only at the last second, during that briefest of moments while he still theoretically continued to exist, had he cried out in a high-pitched voice: "*Pitié!*"† It was the word that he had been searching for all this time, the word he had probably wanted to say for some while. But of course it was now devoid of all meaning—just as any other word would

*   Courage!
†   Mercy!

have been. *"C'est ainsi qu'il a payé sa dette à la société."** Thus
ended the article on his execution. And for the last time
I thought about what society had given him: a fortuitous
birth into poverty and drunkenness, a hungry childhood,
work in the slaughterhouses, tuberculosis, the withered
bodies of several prostitutes, then Lida and the wretched
temptation of wealth, then a murder so inextricably linked
to the terrible poverty of his own imagination, and then,
finally, after months of imprisonment, a cold breeze one
autumn morning, the walkway to the guillotine, a little
rum and one last cigarette before dying. Such as he was,
he would have been incapable of living any other life, and
this life had now reached its logical conclusion. Had he not
committed the murder he would have died of consumption, and on this point his advocate, naturally, had been
correct. One thing was clear: that there was no longer any
room for him in this world, as if the huge expanse of the
Earth's surface had suddenly closed in on him.

I read about his execution in the morning papers the
following day. For some time now I had been living in Rue
Molitor, in the apartment where Pavel Alexandrovich had
been killed, the deeds to which, as it became clear when
putting his affairs in order, he had bought shortly before
his death. I had rearranged the furniture and replaced
the wallpaper and the rugs; where the piano previously
stood there was now a large radio set; I had also got rid

* It is in so doing that he has paid his debt to society.

of the writing desk and replaced it with another, much bigger, one with sliding drawers. Only the armchair and the bookshelves remained exactly as they were before, in the very same spots. I had carefully examined the entire library at leisure and found it to be comprised almost exclusively of the classics—in this sense Pavel Alexandrovich had been a man of his time, and there were very few books by contemporary authors. What seemed even more astonishing to me was that he had almost no personal documents, aside from several letters sent to him many years ago bearing the address of a hotel on Rue de Buci, where he must have been living in those days. One letter was written in a woman's hand, and when I saw it, my eyes were immediately drawn to the words: "You haven't forgotten, I hope, those moments…" I felt pained and uncomfortable, so I put the letter away without reading it. Then there was the single letter he received from his brother, the one who had drowned, leaving to Pavel Alexandrovich his entire fortune; of this one I read every word. It was, however, very brief and almost unprecedented in its bluntness. It ended thus:

"Thank God you know me well and know that I have always preferred to speak the truth than to linger on sentimental nonsense. That you are my brother is an accident of birth, for which I am by no means responsible. The life you have led or are leading is of no interest to me; that is your own affair. I do not know you, nor do I wish to. In the coming days I shall be leaving here for another country, so please do not take it upon yourself to search for me or to write to me. I wish you every kindness, but you must not expect anything of me. That much you already know, I am certain."

These words, the idiotic severity of which seemed utterly inconceivable, were followed by the unexpected signature: "Your loving brother Nikolai". This man had a peculiar understanding of certain words, and I wondered whether he had recollected anyone's love as it dawned on him that he was drowning and that everything was at an end.

There were no photographs, no documents other than a passport issued in Constantinople in 191—, containing a French visa, and a Parisian *carte d'identité* inscribed with the words: bachelor, no occupation. I learnt that Pavel Alexandrovich had been born in Smolensk, but the intervening years between the date of his birth and the date stamped in his passport were a total blank—no papers, no photographs, no mention at all of what he had been doing or where he had been. Then came a second interval, also very lengthy—his whole life in Paris, equally as empty and unknown as the one that had preceded it— for, as the Gentleman had told me, Pavel Alexandrovich had turned up on Rue Simon le Franc only two years before I first met him in the Jardin du Luxembourg. And so I mused on the fact that I knew practically nothing about the man to whom fate had bound me in such a strange and unexpected manner; those images fixed in my memory—first the picturesque beggar, then the dapper, self-assured elderly man—began to seem to me at times almost arbitrary, like the false, phantom shadows of the world that had torn my own life in half, the world I was now trying to forget. Ever since the day I stepped out of that prison, not once had I sensed its vague approach; it was as if it had vanished.

However, as it so happened I was not the only one to wonder about Pavel Alexandrovich's fate. One day, completely by chance, I ran into the Gentleman, who extended his dark hand with its blackened nails and shook my own for such for a long time, looking at me so expressly that I had no alternative but to invite him to a café. This was near Boulevard Saint-Michel. I asked him what he wanted to drink, and he replied that he never drank anything other than red wine. He then began telling me how the course of my life reminded him, albeit in a different way, of the princess's, who naturally… But there I stopped him, and he proceeded to talk about Shcherbakov. It was astonishing how the latter's tragic demise inspired in the Gentleman a sort of posthumous veneration of his memory, as he no longer referred to him as "Pashka Shcherbakov" but rather "the late Pavel Alexandrovich". On that day he seemed drawn for some reason to reflecting on a number of abstract themes.

"Now see here," he said. "What a strange affair all this has been: Pavel Alexandrovich dies, and you receive the inheritance. But who are you? I've the greatest respect for you, but you're still a complete nobody who's turned up from God only knows where."

"Yes, that's quite true."

"But," he went on, "where did the late Pavel Alexandrovich get his fortune before that? From his late brother who drowned in the sea. To think, what a tragedy it must have been for him."

"Yes, I know."

"No, no. You see, the point is this: it wouldn't have mattered if one of us had drowned."

"Well, I don't know about that…"

"No, I mean that drowning in itself is no great pity. If you drown, you drown, and that's that. But what does the brother think of as he drowns? My God, he thinks, all that money! Yet he drowns all the same. Very well, so be it. But where did he get that fortune of his? From his parents, no doubt. And whatever became of them? No one remembers their deaths. So just look how it all turns out: some people who died long ago once had a fortune, which was inherited by their eldest son—he drowned. It then passed to their youngest—he was murdered. Correct? And so the deceased parents' money goes to you—and when they died you probably hadn't even been born. That, as they say, is the face of capitalism for you."

"Are you against the capitalist system?"

"Who? Me?" he exclaimed. "Me? Kostya Voronov? I defended it with a gun in my hands. The dispatch read: 'Distinguished himself through unflinching bravery, setting an example to his commanding officers and subordinates alike…' That's how I fought for capitalism. And if the need arises again, then again I'll go into battle, you may rest assured. No, I meant only that it was you who got the inheritance. By His grace it fell to you, though more's the pity it wasn't to me."

"Well, what would you have done with it?"

"I'd have taken an apartment opposite hers. In the evening I would have gone to her window and said, 'Well then, my little princess, hmm?' I can just imagine her face."

He drank glass after glass and started rambling; his every word now concerned only the princess. I finally managed to escape, my ultimate thought being that his earlier ruminations had nevertheless contained a paradoxical, though undeniable, grain of truth. Then I purchased a few books and returned home.

It was strange to think that I was living in an apartment where a murder had been committed, although I did not dwell on it and was rather disposed to forget it. After a while the apartment began to seem no different from any other, and what prevailed was its peculiar, almost austere comfort, which neither the spectre of the victim nor that of the murderer could disturb. It somehow invited a degree of regularity, a slow meditative life. I soon found myself living there as if I had stepped into someone else's life, as if I were fifty years old and my relocation had been preceded by a long and wearying existence. In effect, this impression coincided to a certain degree with reality, as the mental exhaustion I suffered was beyond doubt. For instance, I could no longer read a book that demanded any degree of focus, and every time my mind reached a crucial point requiring concentration I would suddenly, in broad daylight, start to feel very drowsy and doze off in the armchair. This state of mental torpor was further intensified by the fact that the material conditions of my life had altered drastically and I no longer had to worry about anything: the money in my possession was deposited in several European banks and I had a current account in Paris; what I had so often dreamt of when I lacked the money to pay for dinner in a restaurant or even a pack of cigarettes had now come true. Back then I had wanted to travel, dreaming at night of cabins on board transatlantic liners, of game and lobster, of wagon-lit compartments, of Italy, California and far-away islands, of moonlight dancing on the ocean, of the gentle lapping of nocturnal waves and the vague charm of an unfamiliar melody in my ears. But now, when all I had to do in order to realize any one of these plans was to pick up the telephone, make a couple of enquiries and purchase a ticket, I found that I hadn't the slightest inclination to do it.

I rarely thought about all this, but when I did I could never quite escape the idea that again, completely by chance, as so often happened with me, I was living the life of another man, the reality of which seemed as little convincing to me as did the cheques I signed, the money in my accounts, and this trove of enormous, valuable objects that surrounded me in my apartment on Rue Molitor.

I would go to bed late and I would rise late; I would take a warm bath, which further weakened me, drink a leisurely cup of coffee, get dressed, read the newspaper— for which I had little patience—and think that I had not been to university in some time, and that the course, not a single lecture of which I had attended, would soon be over. But university, too, now seemed entirely unnecessary to me. Then I would sit at the table with its starched linen tablecloth and take lunch, served by Marie, that same woman who worked for Pavel Alexandrovich, who tries to tell me for the hundredth time how she turned the key in the lock, opened the door, went in and immediately spotted blood on the rug and thought that there must have been some sort of disaster.

"I soon knew it! It didn't take me long to realize. My God, I thought, something awful has happened to poor *Monsieur Tcherliakoff*."

She had a habit of butchering his difficult Slavic surname, but always in the same way, so that it came out something like Tcherliakoff.

After lunch I would go into the study, where she would bring me another cup of coffee; I would go over to the shelves, take the first book I came across and begin to read it, although I would presently close it and sit down in the armchair, my mind blank. Only on the rarest of occasions, once every two or three weeks, always unexpectedly, at night or during the day, would I suddenly hear someone's distant voice:

But come you back when all the flow'rs are dying,
If I am dead—as dead I well may be—
You'll come and find the place where I am lying…

and then I would hurriedly open the book and with rapt attention read every word and every line aloud.

Sometimes I would go to the cinema, but even that drained me. I continued to live mostly in that same quiet torpor, and no matter what occupied my thoughts nothing seemed to merit any effort on my part. Never before had I been so strangely and completely aware of my loneliness. During the course of several months I received three letters: one was an invitation to dinner from some acquaintances whose daughter I had instructed in French for a short while; the two others were from friends. I did not reply to any of them, however, and stopped receiving post entirely. A few times I visited the Latin Quarter, where I had lived for four years and knew each and every building, but it seemed somehow foreign and distant to me—as if the man who had lived there had imparted all his many optical impressions to me, haphazardly detaching them from their emotional reverberations, without which they had lost all meaning and significance. From time to time I began to think that Shcherbakov's inheritance had perhaps never really been meant for me, although I now knew why he had made out a will in my favour—but that, too, had been the result of a misunderstanding. Before they came from the furniture shop to bring the new writing desk and to remove the old one, I found several sheets of paper that had been mislaid in the right-hand drawer. Among them was a thick envelope that had been torn in half, on which was written in pencil: "*Mk. wl. in fav. of stud. in grat. for 10 fr.*"—"Make will in favour of the student, in gratitude for the ten francs", those ten francs that I had given him in the Jardin du Luxembourg. He never knew that I had simply been unable to act otherwise, I had no choice but to do so. There was one more week until the end of the month, when I was to receive my stipend, and I had only two bank notes in my wallet: one hundred-franc note and another for ten francs. That was all the money I had; I couldn't have given him the hundred francs, but nor did I have the option to give him less than ten. It was a minor financial misunderstanding that had given him a false impression of my supposed munificence: what he had taken for generosity was simply a consequence of my poverty. And so I was indebted to this glaring error of judgement for everything I now possessed; Kostya Voronov had been right to say, "But you're still a complete nobody who's turned up from God only knows where." This off-hand remark, uttered by a drunken beggar, was a very succinct and totally accurate description, although naturally the Gentleman had in no way desired to express in the most precise terms possible what it was that comprised the pitiful singularity of my existence.

Winter returned with its piercing cold and winds; its dry, frozen dust swept along the street and with a light rustle came to rest in the road and on the pavement. One day, having managed to shake off that persistent mental inertia to which I had become so accustomed, I stepped out into the street and headed for the Bois de Boulogne. It was peaceful and deserted there; its alleys were strewn with fallen leaves, the air bore the faint smell of frozen earth and the wind was chasing ripples across the surface of the cold, empty lakes. For two hours I slowly wandered around the park; then, long after it had grown dark and the hazy light of the street lamps had appeared, I returned home. Dinner was ready and there was red wine on the table, which Marie persisted in serving with every meal, although I never touched a drop. That evening, however, after the long walk, I poured myself a glass for the first time and drank it up there and then; the wine was strong and quite sweet, and it tasted rather pleasant.

After dinner the table was cleared, and Marie bade me

good night and left. Now alone, I moved into the study, where I sat down in the armchair, unsure of what do with myself, my mind blank. Quite by chance my eyes came to rest on the desk calendar, which Marie religiously changed each day. It was 11 February. I had a vague recollection that this date was in some way significant. Perhaps it was linked to some historical event that had at some point and for some reason drawn my attention.

All of a sudden it hit me—and I felt ashamed that it had taken me so long to remember. On this evening exactly one year ago, in this study where I was now sitting, Pavel Alexandrovich had been murdered.

I stood up from the armchair, selected a book from the shelf and opened it.

> *Et ces mêmes fureurs que vous me dépeignez,*
> *Ces bras que dans le sang vous avez vus baignés…**

No, I was in no mood for *Iphigénie*. I extracted a second book, again at random; it was the famous *Diary of Samuel Pepys*.

> To the King's Theatre, where we saw *Midsummer's Night's Dream*, which I had never seen before, nor shall ever again, for it is the most insipid, ridiculous play that ever I saw in my life.

---

* And these same furies you describe to me, / These arms you have seen bathed in blood…

I replaced the book on its shelf. Despite my efforts, I was thinking about that date in February, about what had immediately preceded it and what had followed. Then I raised my eyes to the bookshelf above me. Everything was just as it had been a year ago: the same order, the same spines, and in front of them, in the middle of the bookshelf, the golden Buddha with its forever still, ecstatic face. As I looked at it, I recalled the words of the investigator:

"If we can find the statuette, you'll be free to return home…"

I picked up the Buddha and examined it with a complex feeling that was difficult to describe. Still, it was impossible to forget that its return had brought about my freedom. It was the very same Buddha that Amar's swarthy hands had gripped, that later would stand in the prostitute's room, surrounded by cloudlets of cheap scent, that had travelled in the investigator's leather briefcase, and whose appearance or disappearance had meant many other things, and in particular that none of the events connected with its return, none of the shifting emotions, none of the attempts to understand it, would ever explain the true meaning of its mysterious exaltation, just as no number of years in the Louvre could explain the composition of the soul of the long-dead artist who had painted the ecstasy of St Jerome.

The lamplight was falling on the statuette, as I just stood there staring at it. Outside, the window was covered in evening frost. Only the desk lamp in the study was lit, and the walls and furniture loomed dimly out of the dark shadows. A still silence reigned all around.

I kept looking at the Buddha, and suddenly I saw its face blur and disappear in a fraction of a second, leaving a yellow spot where it had only just been, which was imperceptibly growing larger and taking up more and more space. Then it outgrew the room, its features vanished, and in that same instant I realized that a musical motif, strangely combining a guitar and a violin, had been ringing in my ears all this time. I recognized it, but was unable to remember how it went, and I kept trying to recall, fitfully and in vain, where I had heard it and when. At the end of the long yellow vista that had imperceptibly appeared before me, at an extraordinary and improbable distance, several rounded steps led up to a stage, atop which, gleaming tragically, there was a grand piano with an elderly man in tails sitting at it. To my right, a man walked past, taking very slow steps, noiselessly, as in a dream; the lapels of his smoking jacket looked as if they had been moulded onto his starched chest. His face was so familiar to me that at any other time there could have been no mistaking it, but now it seemed as if my memory was barely able to register these visual impressions; I made a phenomenal effort and it suddenly dawned on me that the face was that of the Gentleman. A ruddy young man in glasses passed me on my left, leading an elderly woman by the arm; around her wrinkled neck were several loops of an enormous pearl necklace. I seemed to recognize her too; I had seen that dancing, youthful gait—surprising in a woman of her advanced years—somewhere before. The hall was gradually and just as silently filling with people in evening dress, and I seemed to recognize acquaintances in every one of them, by their forgotten gestures or facial expressions. I then looked up at the wall, above the heads of the crowd, and suddenly a chill ran through me. I had no idea how it had got there, but it was the same mountain landscape, the memory of which I had borne through that far-away death. I recognized the sheer cliff face with its ledges and little bushes; the broken branch of a dead tree was clearly visible. More cliffs rose up on both sides, forming an enormous pit. Below, with his left arm off to one side and his right bent under him, on the stony bank of the rapid, narrow river lay the corpse of a man in brown mountaineering attire.

I took a step backward, but behind me there was a soft velvet wall. I looked about, then cast my eyes towards the source of all these people, where by all accounts there ought to have been a door. However, there was no door; in its place, rising up almost the entire height of the wall, hung an enormous wood-block portrait of a man with a low forehead, dressed in a semi-military jacket that was decorated with various medals.

Just then—the hall was nearly full now—there was an almighty crash and a thunderous din. Male and female voices merged into one booming mass, among which it was possible at times to make out individual phrases in several different languages. Then a hush descended over everything, and in the unexpected pause there was a heavy cracking sound immediately followed by a death rattle. Someone fell over in the middle of the hall and a crowd immediately gathered; however, at that moment the pianist, who had until now been sitting at the piano with strange, unflinching stillness, began playing some peculiarly raucous dance motif, which was presently taken up by a violin and a guitar. Then the amorphous racket began to abate, and the piano, too, began to sound more and more distant; after a few seconds there was silence once again. Next, slowly distancing itself from me in this expansive vista, the silhouette of a tall man in a navy-blue suit passed by, moving about the murky air with none of the hesitation that is natural for anyone walking about in the dark. He went up onto the stage, vanished and immediately reappeared, whereupon I seemed to catch his cold, limpid gaze. His inexpressive voice reached over to me, uttering a short fragment that I couldn't make out. He spoke these words and disappeared. Shortly thereafter, I became doubly and blindly aware of what was going on, and I was momentarily struck by a sense that there was no escape or any means of combating this—other than with some brief combination of magic words, which I did not know and which perhaps did not exist at all. I looked about myself in despair, and amid the yellowish twilight of the hall, through the misty shadows, I distinctly spotted a face with a typical Arabian profile, dead, black eyes and trembling lips. The sound of the piano came again from the stage. I looked over; beside the pianist, in a white ball gown that fitted her waist tightly at the middle, stood a woman with heavy eyes. A moment later I heard her deep voice, but the stage suddenly retreated into the distance so that the sound grew weak and I was unable to make out either the melody or the words of her song. A minute passed by, then another—and finally the voice started to draw nearer again, carrying with it its own melodic power. I caught only the last verse, and I felt a familiar pain in the left side of my chest as I remembered another voice, light, pure and crystalline—Catherine's voice, which had so often sung those very words:

And I shall hear though soft you tread above me,
And all my grave shall warmer, sweeter be,
For you shall bend and tell me that you love me
And I shall sleep in peace until you come to me.

Instantly my breathing became laboured, and again all the muscles in my body contracted to the point of pain; I was vaguely aware that my entire future and all its potential rested on surviving this final, inconceivable onslaught. And so, with astounding slowness, the view of the hall gradually became narrower, the yellowish light grew darker by degrees and, after several minutes of this agonizing torment, before me appeared the murky features of my study, the Buddha's golden face and the pale fingers of my hand, clutching the statuette so tightly that they were in pain. My forehead was damp with perspiration and I felt a weight in my head, but this seemed entirely immaterial and inconsequential in comparison with the wild sense of freedom I felt, as for the first time ever I was indebted for my victory over this illusory world not to some external jolt or fortuitous awakening, but to the strength of my own will.

From the next day onward I began a new life, completely different from the one I had been leading until now. In the mornings I would take cold showers instead of warm baths, and then I would head off to university. I would sometimes go to the cinema or to a cabaret, from which I would return on foot in the cold February night, taking in the frosty air. On returning home I would always sleep soundly.

*   *   *

One morning I received a letter—in a thick blue envelope bearing an Australian postage stamp.

"Why did you take so long to come and see me in Paris? I waited for you so. You now know everything that happened in the wake of your needless disappearance. The man I married left me to go to England, and I have sent the divorce papers to him. I cannot return to Europe because of my financial situation, and I know that you too have no money for the journey to Melbourne. But perhaps we shall meet again one day, and now I am prepared to wait for you my whole life.

"Do you remember that sentimental song I taught you? 'Oh, Danny Boy!' Every time I remember the melody I think of you and feel like crying."

Several days later I left for Australia. And as I watched the receding shores of France from the ship's deck, I thought that among the mass of equally arbitrary speculations as to what this journey and the Buddha's return had meant for me, as well as what the true meaning of my own fate had been in these last few years, it was perhaps worth allowing for the possibility that it had been just the gruelling wait for this long sea voyage—a wait whose significance I had been unable to fathom until the last minute.

PUSHKIN PRESS

Pushkin Press was founded in 1997, and publishes novels, essays, memoirs, children's books—everything from timeless classics to the urgent and contemporary.

This book is part of the Pushkin Collection of paperbacks, designed to be as satisfying as possible to hold and to enjoy. It is typeset in Monotype Baskerville, based on the transitional English serif typeface designed in the mideighteenth century by John Baskerville. It was litho-printed on Munken Premium White Paper and notch-bound by the independently owned printer TJ International in Padstow, Cornwall. The cover, with French flaps, was printed on Colorplan Pristine White paper. The paper and cover board are both acid-free and Forest Stewardship Council (FSC) certified.

Pushkin Press publishes the best writing from around the world—great stories, beautifully produced, to be read and read again.

STEFAN ZWEIG · EDGAR ALLAN POE · ISAAC BABEL
TOMÁS GONZÁLEZ · ULRICH PLENZDORF · TEFFI
VELIBOR ČOLIĆ · LOUISE DE VILMORIN · MARCEL AYMÉ
ALEXANDER PUSHKIN · MAXIM BILLER · JULIEN GRACQ
BROTHERS GRIMM · HUGO VON HOFMANNSTHAL
GEORGE SAND · PHILIPPE BEAUSSANT · IVÁN REPILA
E.T.A. HOFFMANN · ALEXANDER LERNET-HOLENIA
YASUSHI INOUE · HENRY JAMES · FRIEDRICH TORBERG
ARTHUR SCHNITZLER · ANTOINE DE SAINT-EXUPÉRY
MACHI TAWARA · GAITO GAZDANOV · HERMANN HESSE
LOUIS COUPERUS · JAN JACOB SLAUERHOFF
PAUL MORAND · MARK TWAIN · PAUL FOURNEL
ANTAL SZERB · JONA OBERSKI · MEDARDO FRAILE
HÉCTOR ABAD · PETER HANDKE · ERNST WEISS
PENELOPE DELTA · RAYMOND RADIGUET · PETR KRÁL
ITALO SVEVO · RÉGIS DEBRAY · BRUNO SCHULZ